A BEGINNING TO AN END

Darimbari

Sudha Madhuri D.

KNOWLEDGE WORLD

KW Publishers Pvt Ltd

New Delhi

2011   BEST PUBLISHERS AWARD (ENGLISH)

KNOWLEDGE WORLD

KW Publishers Pvt Ltd

4676/21, First Floor, Ansari Road, Daryaganj, New Delhi 110002

Email: knowledgeworld@vsnl.net Tel.: +91.11.23263498/43528107

www.kwpub.com

This novel is a work of fiction, it bears no resemblance to anyone dead or alive.

ISBN 978-93-81904-35-0

For my daughters...........Rishika who wants a horse.
Abhilasha who wants me to write another dream.
And Rishanjali who is quite unaware of what is going on.

Contents

1. The Beginning

It was a hot, sultry afternoon. Flies, foul body odour, and dry cough was all playing loudly on Beral Chandra Ghanadas's audio and olfactory senses. The buses of Kolkata, plying in heavy traffic are enough to give jittery nerves to the well-healed travellers among us. Beral Babu often felt engulfed by these red beasts. There was a deep overwhelming sense of no escape from the routine of 8 to 5 job in the Swadhin Bank, and thrown in as a bonus, of course, was the jostling ride from home to the bank and back.

He had a scooter—his father-in-law's benevolence—that still had brand new tyres. Beral Babu suffered from road fear; even driving to the grocery shop of Agarwal bania just round the corner of his home required gladiator's preparation.

One could not call him a brave heart; yet, his daily travels in the red beast entitled him to the rank of a dare heart. Beral Babu had never ever broken this routine other than Sundays. On this day, wherever he had to go and whatever he had to do was done on man's two best friends—his bipedal, I would say, he was a foot soldier at heart.

At the office, Beral Babu's name was often mispronounced as 'Biral' (cat) by some of his colleagues who thought being comical in a government institution brought more lightness into the dank morbid atmosphere of a dusty government building.

Harish Ghosh, the Bada Babu of the clerical section, would say with a lot of humour, "Now that Biral has turned up, we can all meow to our work."

Beral Babu, on such occasions, would say nothing but move to his desk and turn deaf ears. He did feel bad about the fun being made at his expense but confrontation was not a part of his sweet nature.

Work! I would say happened at a slow pace, soft-footed I would rather say, with a number of intermittent tea breaks, and those who did not drink this savvy beverage, would make trips to the toilets or take pan breaks in the long corridor of the office building that was lined with low wooden benches (had vital parts missing and had seen better days during the British Raj).

Lunch break 1 'o' clock; it seemed as if the whole world of the babus had come to a standstill; the old government building of the bank ceased to show any notable life forms. Every vacant chair reminded one of this advanced breed among mankind who had dedicated their lives to the improvement of the whole human race.

A closer look revealed hardworking babus in the lunchroom cooling their belly fires. Tiffin opened, spoons raised and naked fingers readied like gladiators, their hands moving with more alacrity and swiftness of a samurai's sword held ready for a battle than with pens on the office files. The rhythmic clickity-clack of spoons often reminded one of Mozart's orchestra.

Beral Babu's tiffin was the most awaited; it was not only big in size but also ample and filling in contents.

Hot and steaming flavoured rice, juicy fiery fish curry, and small round meatballs in creamy cashew sauce. Often, the small side tiffin contained added treats of malpuas, sandesh, and soft white rasgullas. Most of his colleagues would take the excuse of telling something important at that eventful moment, and would often depart with a prized piece held tenderly between their fingers to be devoured leisurely at their own lunch tables.

Portly, pink-faced and sweet-natured Beral Babu never felt offended; in fact, he felt happy sharing God's bounty with these lesser mortals. Ruti, tarkari, and dal had never been his scene.

He was more of a happy-eating and go-lucky person. The words diet or soups never featured in his menu. Lunch over, the babu's groaned back to their creaking wooden chairs and grunting wooden desks complaining loudly how unfair the government was, and their heavy workload literally was killing them.

Back pain, gas, burps, and hiccups followed the small and big hands of the clock till just about five minutes to five; then the frenzy of activity seen was like piranhas feeding on live bait. Just as the big old dame showed five, the stillness that descended within the office was resounding, hitting one like a full blast of cold air on a mountaintop.

The peon at the gate, old Salaam khan, who has been at his post for the last fifteen years, waited for the office grounds to clear, and then started locking up the old rickety wooden doors with Sriram Ghosh, a young sturdy fellow of just twenty, newly married; he always seemed in a hurry to go home.

Every now and then, between closing doors and shifting chairs, Sriram Ghosh would disappear like a wispy ghost, but of course, a loud hollering from Khan and he would trot back like the wayward donkey of the washerman.

Halfhearted sweeping of the floors was done by the one-eyed maid who lived behind the office building. Khan knew her from the time she was a young bride, when she had two good eyes about two score years back. Unfortunately, her drunk husband decided otherwise... he threw an empty bottle at her and sealed the fate of her brightness.

Fate decides all...was the last thought on Khan's mind as he locked the main gate.

Beral Babu often travelled back in the same bus as Badai da, a resident of Jalpaiguri who had been living out his years in Kolkata as a NRK (Non-Residential Kolkatian); some in the office said he had a tyrant of a wife who did not let him come home.

Beral Babu was a wee bit apprehensive about travelling alone; hence, he had in fact requested Badai da to travel with him in the same bus.

Badai da always had sarcasm dripping of his tongue like honey, yet, he was sometimes very entertaining as he often kept one's mind engaged with tall stories about his wife and her knowledge about running an efficient household, and how cleverly she was bringing up the children even though she herself had never seen the gates of a school.

Getting down at the corner near his house, Beral Babu would trudge back picking up a few fresh vegetables or grocery as per requests from his better half.

Beral Babu's better half—Binodini Kumari—was just twenty and a few odd years more; after so many years of marriage, she had settled into a sweet-natured plump roundness that was often seen during those days among most ginnis (Bengali housewives).

She was still very pretty and the city life hardly had any effect on her inherent nice and kind nature.

"Age is catching up on you, Beral Babu," said Badai da.

"I can see you huffing and puffing just these few steps to the home stead," he said with sarcasm dripping from his lips like warm nectar.

Beral Babu did not like what he heard but like many times before, he behaved as if he had not heard what was being said and shifted to pleasanter topics.

Beral Babu loved food, and his portly comfortableness was an evidence of this fact.

Hilsa fish, a Bengali delicacy, and of course very many ways to cook, it was one of his favourite topics and mood lifters.

"Are you going to buy some today?" asked Badai da.

No, no, no....no," not being very sure, "I will pick up some on Sunday...have to ask Binodini first," he said.

Badai da smirked sarcastically and said, "Always in line with the missus, are we not... huh!"

Beral Babu wanted to reply; he felt hurt too at the unwarranted sarcasm but his years of taking such literary pain from others had trained him to develop an impervious epidermis, and such kind of unworthy words were like water being poured on a drake.

Magically, a net bag would appear from the office satchel to carry the few vegetables and other items on his way home.

Badai da had no such compulsions, as there was no cooking to be done; all he ever ate was bread with mango pickle followed by a glass of tea served by the tea boy. At night, sometimes, he would pour water on some puffed rice and after squeezing the whole lot dry, he would add a pinch of sugar and a squeeze of a sweet lime and lo! his dinner was ready.

At the office, he fell back on the kind mercies of the canteen that served thick brown undercooked rice and watery dal; sometimes on lucky days, there would be a piece of solitary vegetable floating in the watery soup.

Beral Babu, speaking to him and shaking his arm to get his attention, brought him back to the present. "Come over for a cup of tea; Binodini will make some nice mean pakoras." Invitation tendered, Beral Babu waited, already knowing the usual answer.

Badai da's pan-stained lips moved in an irregular manner refusing politely as usual. Both friends parted at the roundel, Beral Babu headed home and Badai da to his one-roomed barsati, which he shared with one of his cousins.

Badai da liked Beral Babu but with plenty of reservations in mind. He often felt jealous of the loving couple; in his envy, he was often rude and sarcastic with the gentle soul, regretting later over his behaviour. Life was lonely and he missed his sons but his wife's behaviour left little room for peace in the house. By choice, he had chosen to live as he did. Although Swadhin Bank did have a branch close to his home, Badai da had never asked for a transfer.

He was a porcupine... always with his hackles raised to fend off imaginary attacks.

As Beral Babu walked home, he met friends who too were returning home after having accomplished similar missions like him.

The very thought of his Binodini and her soft hands serving tea to him cheered him up, and made him forget the earlier feeling of hurt and unkindness.

Beral Babu could never understand why Badai da was so nasty sometimes; innate politeness prevented him from even asking.

Badai da walked into his single room that served as both a bedroom and a sitting room, a sense of disgust and anger arose in him. The whole room was in disarray, dirty clothes, cigarette stubs, and torn pieces of newspaper littered the floor.

A while back, Badai da had divided the room into two halves so that at least his would remain suitable for human habitation; it had never worked. Today, the whole room was worse than a pigsty, and he waited for his cousin to return.

2. Binodini

Binodini was a very nice and sweet-natured woman. Being from a village that was a bit in the interiors, she had only studied up to class four; hence, lacked the swift knowledge and cunningness of city women. Neighbours and friends liked her but often her caring nature was taken advantage of by unscrupulous women…kids of all growing stages would be dumped on her by her friends who wanted a day out in the Victoria Memorial or went to watch a talkie at the Raj Theatre.

Binodini felt bad that none of her friends ever invited her to go along or share their fun at their various shopping expedition. By nature being kind and taught to be polite and subdued to elders, she never ever spoke her mind or showed displeasure.

She often envied some of the women in her neighbourhood, their way of wearing saris, the nice blouses, and their beautiful hairstyles. She would sit in a corner and hear her friends chat about clothes, jewellery and the club … she would soak in all the information wide-eyed.

Suchitra, Mukta, and Sunanda were some of her friends. Whenever they would go anywhere, she would gladly babysit, and later, over cups of tea and pakoras that Binodini would gladly make for them, she would be treated to their tall tales about the outside world. On such days, Binodini would eagerly wait for her husband to come home. Who else in this world would listen patiently to her heard experiences?

The house in which the Berals lived was very old, and had seen better days during Beral Babu's grandfather's era, who had retired as a postmaster. Under Beral Babu's soft fleshy hands, the small wrought iron gate creaked open, protesting on its two last existing hinges.

"Binoo… Binoo oo." The last call was a bit impatient.

Where Was She? ....She Never Took So Long.

Usually, before he could call out for the third time, Binodini would appear without fail at the head of the small wooden staircase with a glass of water in hand and a lovely smile playing on her lips.

She was the brightest star in his life; always waiting for him and him alone. As he slipped on the last staircase and almost tripped over, he was again reminded of the fact that indeed his house needed quite a lot of repair work, some painting, and denting work too.

"Have to speak to Majumdar; remind me later in the evening. The house needs to be painted before the Durga pujo." Binodini, as usual, was always in agreement; she said, "Will do so; you first wash, change, and relax. I will get you a cup of tea and some hot shingaras that I have made for you a little while ago."

The small house had slanting tiled roof of faded red colour, and a small English verandah with a few wrought iron garden chairs that sufficed to entertain visitors.

Beral Babu sat in his favourite armchair and looked lovingly at the bougainvillea that was flowering profusely with a burst of dark pink colour at this time of the year. It gave a very 'English' look to the bungalow-styled house.

"How was your day at the office?"....she always asked this same question, and had been doing so, for years now.

Beral Babu would make light of all that happened in the office and of course Badai da's honey-coated sarcasm.

"He is an old man with half his teeth missing; I feel pity for him.... no matter what, treat him with kindness," said Binodini.

He looked across at Binodini who was shifting her ample proportions in one of the chairs trying to be more comfortable. Been married for almost fifteen odd years now, with his mother's passing away, Binodini had become lonelier and more so since she had no children of her own but.... life never stops; it goes on and on.

"Sunanda and Sharmistha had come... they had gone to see a talkie, story is so interesting, just listen ...what happens is that..." Beral Babu smiled indulgently and listened most attentively to his wife's tall tales and small incidents from her day's routine.

Life for them was simple; Binodini believed in doing all her own work and Beral Babu did his bit of a handyman's job on Sundays... a little straightening of the small garden, changing bulbs...Beral Babu hated all kinds of physical exertion; it made him tired but to make his Binoo happy, he would always put up a show.

The rooms of the house were small but airy; two small bedrooms and a toilet, the house had an ancient well in the courtyard.

Often on Sunday mornings, Beral Babu preferred taking a bath in the courtyard. Binodini would make sure he had ample cold fresh water to take a bath in. What more could one wish for in life!

He would often carry back old newspapers from the office, which on those special Sundays, he would read out from, telling Binodini about all the interesting happenings in the world. She would listen wide-eyed and ask many questions. Sometimes in the evening, they would listen to records on the gramophone.

Beral Babu just about had one vice...listening to songs on the gramophone.

Another harried day at the office...Saturday was always the busiest as Sunday was just round the corner. Beral Babu, in his corner seat, was trying to finish his pile of files for the day. Just then, Debendra Ghosh, the senior clerk of their section approached Beral Babu's desk, small end of his dhuti in his left hand, smiling countenance, pan stained uneven teeth; everyone in the office said he had a thick tongue.... Beral Babu could never understand the meaning of such a pun as Ghosh was not only quick-witted but spoke very well too.

"Ki Beral Babu, what are your plans?" he said with a questioning look....Beral Babu was a little puzzled on hearing such an obtuse and unrelated question but replied, "Plans? What plans?"

"Kyano…. pujo plans! Are you not planning anything? Going anywhere, think of boudi also," there was a loud smirk on Debendra Ghosh's face. To tell the truth, between smirks and laughs, Beral Babu had no plans at all; after all, life for him was going on nicely; why upset the already set routines?

Anyway, he had to give some reply to the nosy Debendra Ghosh; hence, he said, "I am planning to take her to the Pujo Bari of course…. Some new clothes…. Mishti…." The very thought of mishti clouded Beral Babu's eyes with sweet emotions and his tongue coated with a sea of dreamy waves. Ghosh shook his head like a rattlesnake and said, "Dada, not happening at all …. not fair, I am planning to go to Puri; if you want you can join us, the more the merrier."

Beral Babu did not give any answer; instead, he called out to Sanatan, the office tea boy to get two cups. Ghosh adjusted the folds of his dhuti, plunked himself on one of the rickety chairs, and slurped from the saucer loudly giving intermittent breaks to blow heavily on the surface of the hot liquid to cool it down. Ghosh was not only irritating but also extremely thick skinned.

Before departing, Ghosh asked Beral Babu to give it a thought and let him know, for reservations in Puri Express are difficult to get at this time of the year but since his wife's brother was working in the reservation counter, it sometime helped.

While in the belly of the red beast Badai da was unusually quiet that day as they got down at the corner. Beral Babu asked him whether he was going home. Badai da looked at him through his best eye, the other being a squint and out of focus, as one never knew what he was looking at or referring to. Taking time to swallow the massive amount of sweet pan juice in his mouth, he somehow managed, "Yes I am…. going home for the pujo; have to pick up a few things for the kids and wife."

Beral Babu observed his friend's glum face…. no sign of happiness there. A few days back, someone in the office did mention about Badai da's bossy wife who had a nasty temper like the Kolkata Tongas....Real Sharp woman.

He was lucky in that aspect, with Binodini in his life who was sweet, soft and gentle....absolutely no demands or wants in life. This time, for the pujo, he would buy her a white sari with a thicker red border.... She would paint a very pretty picture.

Picking up a nice hilsa fish, Beral Babu trudged home. Another blissful weekend, lazing about in the small garden with numerous cups of tea, hot savouries, and of course, the Sunday newspaper... Binodini would be waiting hands on, fulfilling his every tiny wish and whims. What more can a man ask for in his life!

Sitting cross-legged on the mat, Beral Babu separated fish from bone with great care, and stuffed it into his mouth with his thick fleshy fingers as Binodini looked on lovingly, his heavy jowl moved chewing the delicate fish and his cheeks turned red from the heat of the curry; she kept fanning her husband lovingly with a hand fan.

She asked him indulgently, "Shall I give you some more curry and the head of the fish? I still have three more pieces left."

In answer, Beral Babu just shook his thick-matted head, which no amount of oil could keep in place.

Binodini was reminded of her mother-in-law who would ask her to oil her grey head of matted hair....she would try all kinds of magic potions and oils from neem hakims. Though the old woman had the appearance of a shaggy dog, her temper was nothing like one.

Dinner over, sweet pan taken from loving hands, he sat on the bed watching his wife partake of whatever was left after he had eaten. What luck to have found such a nice woman. To tell the truth, there were many proposals for Beral Babu but his mother wanted a simple village girl who would serve one and all willingly; hence, of course, Binodini was the right choice—less educated, a village simpleton who even after having lived for so many years in a big city, had not lost her old-world charms, for which she had been selected as the ideal bride in the first place.

She eats whatever her husband eats, wore what he got for her, and believed what her friends told her. A charmed woman of the new world, I must say.

Gullible Binodini had a heart of gold…. no unhappy and hungry living form was ever turned away from her doorstep empty handed. She had empathy for all.

Repeated ringing of the bell of a cycle rickshaw in the small cobbled road and a loud nasal cry, "Sari le lo…. sari"…. bore sweet music to the ears of all women of the colony.

Binodini was cutting bitter gourd and brinjal to make 'sukto' for Beral Babu, his favourite on Thursdays….supposed to purify his blood…. but there is a big difference between what was being heard, what was being said, and what is to be believed. Beral Babu's large pimples and boils on his face totally negated the idea of the purifying effect of such bitter food, but her mother-in-law had always insisted on sukto on Thursdays, and Binodini still followed old dictums.

Anyway, all said and done, even though she did not believe in the effectiveness of sukto for clearing boils and pimples, yet, she always did that which made him happy.

"Binoo…. aee…Binoo, come out… come quickly." Hearing Suchitra calling, Binodini quickly shut the boat-shaped boti and kept the uncut vegetables aside, hurriedly wiping her hands in the aanchol of her red-bordered white sari; she rushed out.

At Suchitra's house, the sari merchant had already displayed his wares on a mat; Sunanda and a few other neighbourhood women had also gathered.

The feel of new sari, whether cotton or silk, was wonderful and the smell was just heavenly…..handmade treasure on display. Binodini was as excited as her friends, but there is a big divide between liking and being able to take what one likes.

She was at a disadvantage compared to her friends; she had never got that choice to take independent decisions of any kind ever in her life.

The feel of new saris ooh!....ooh! Just as good as having a full rasgulla tossed into the mouth. The riot of colours, borders, and patterns drove a sense of wanted frenzy among the women.

Tinkling of bangles, soft jingling of payals was music to the ear of Mukund Kumar, the sari seller. Selling saris for so many years, he never could make up his mind about getting married.... seeing so many different varieties of women....he was very confused!

He had been coming to this para (neighbourhood) for the last sixteen years or so, seeing these women growing old in his saris but there was always this quiet one who would lovingly see his wares but never ever bought one; he could make out from the excitement in her eyes and the red glow on her cheeks that she liked the red sari very much for she kept touching it.... but ....he knew in his heart that she would not be buying it.

Suchitra picked up a green sari with a nice golden border, it had a lovely motif of peacocks on the aanchol, Tara a pink one, some others chose yellow and some blue; all through this activity, Binodini sat quietly, watching her friends make their choices.

She helped some of her friends to choose too...what looked nice and what suited their complexion.

She liked the red sari very much but then, liking was fine, taking was impossible. These saris were expensive and beyond her meager savings that she kept aside from her monthly household expenditure.

She quietly got up and left; none of her friends even noticed her leaving but for one.

Mukund Kumar did see her leaving like so many times before.

Binodini sat for quite some time in the verandah. She could still hear excited voices floating down from Suchitra's house.

Her mind made an imaginary trip from her early childhood in

the village to her coming to Kolkata as a newlywed bride; life back then had been full of choices and freedom....now she wished she had followed in the steps of her elder sister, life would have been different....could have become a school teacher, a nurse at the government hospital like her sister, then life would have been full of choices and independence.

Today, Beral Babu was late, and Binodini was a little worried for it was very unlike him. She waited anxiously wondering the reason for his delay.

It was much, much later that she heard the clank of the wrought iron gate being opened, and Beral Babu walking in with a big smile on his large face. He held a small package, which he thrust into her hands. "Take a look Binoo, what I have got for you.... I am sure you are going to like it."

After having washed and changed, he sat down on his favourite easy chair with a cup of hot steaming tea in his hand watching his wife picking up his clothes and keeping them in the cupboard.

He looked at the still unopened package lying on the small round table. "Will you not take a look at what is inside?" Seeing her unresponsive face, he wandered what was wrong.... he could not fathom the reason for her sadness.

"Is everything all right?" Even with his kind of gentle coaxing she would not give him an answer.

"All ...fine," was all that she mumbled as she continued to keep up pretenses of doing one or the other chores.

Trying to cheer her up, he tried to make frivolous conversation about his day at the office, that Badai da was going home to his bossy wife and how the prices of everything had sky rocketed... how will the middle class Babu survive. "I had gone to the market with Badai da today and suddenly, I saw this beautiful sari, which I knew would look good on you; open the packet please and see for yourself."

Reluctantly, Binodini started to unwrap the brown paper packet she already knew what it held—the creamy white, well-starched, red bordered sari had a single line of gold on the aanchol. Her back was turned to her husband who was very anxiously waiting for her reaction that was never to come.

His eyes suddenly fell on the dressing table mirror and he saw the sad reflection of her face. With a look of disinterest, she tore the brown paper packet into bits and pieces, and threw it into the dustbin. She did not even pay a second glance to the creamy white fabric in her hands…..his heart froze at her lack of interest.

Binodini so very lost in her own thoughts, little knowing the hurt she had caused to her husband.

Taking a deep breath, she turned around and said, "Nice," just once.

She opened the old wooden cupboard next to the bed and tossed the sari onto the heap of similar such ones. She left the room in silence…. not a word…. not a glance. Beral Babu sat quietly soaking in the silence of the room finding it difficult to even breathe; in so many years, it never struck him even once that Binodini never liked the saris that he got for her.

His tea ran cold sitting on the side table as he sat there thinking for quite sometime, silence being his only company.

During dinner that night, Binodini was trying to be unusually very, very cheerful. After having seen her behaviour earlier in the evening, Beral Babu kept a close watch answering only in monosyllables.

She informed her husband about the day's events, the visit of the sariwala, the choices her friends had made, how exiting her day had been indeed. Beral Babu listened quietly saying a 'yes' or a 'no' wherever necessary but that lively cheerfulness that existed between the couple was missing, and one could feel the strain the mere visit of Mukund Kumar, the sariwala, had put on their dinner conversation.

That night, Beral Babu sat for a while in the small verandah (his usual practice of many years) lost in his thoughts; somewhere he had lost track to his small cozy world, the visit of the sariwala had spoilt his day. May be it was still not too late to do a bit of salvaging work.

One could feel the pujo in the air, a feel of festivity that was to come, new shops had sprung up on both sides of the main road almost overnight selling mounds of mishti of all varieties rasgullas, sandesh, payesh, rasmalai, and many more, not to mention the swarm of flies that arose from these sweet heaps each time the Mithaiwala waved his hands.

Binodini stood coyly next to her husband noticing some of his favourite snacks... shingaras, pyaazi and bora.... "Ashun na, Babu moshai.... come taste my sweets... they are as fresh as a pretty maidens cheeks." Binodini, her aanchol drawn over her head, heard the shopkeeper asking her, "Boudi, what sweets would you like me to pack for you? All are freshly made." He was waiting for her to give some answer.

She wanted to buy some pantuas; they looked nice and juicy, steaming in their own fragrant syrup but in her many years of marriage, she had realised that her in-laws never liked any kind of fried sweets and such supposed taste buds run in the family from one generation to the next.

As far as Beral Babu was concerned, the sight of so many of his favourite mishtis was simply a mouthwatering experience (of course, turning blind eyes to the many different species of flies visiting these huge mounds of sweets) that brought sweet taste of joy, and he was literally being rendered into a speechless rhapsody.

What to buy and what not to buy was a difficult choice but the mithaiwala Sen Sharma knew Beral Babu's taste well. He had seen him grow from boyhood to manhood, his large size was all thanks to his sweets and spicy savouries. Beral Babu just could manage to point out, what he wanted and it was very difficult for him to speak, as his mouth was full of saliva. At the end, there were quite a few packages in their hands. Beral Babu hired a cycle rickshaw of uncertain balance and perching on the small seat, they made their way home, he quite happy thinking of the happy sweet days ahead and she still thinking about the lack of capacity to make choices in life.

3. A Meeting of Great Minds

The rickshawala was straining, grunting and groaning trying to make lightning speed with his not-so-light passengers; poor man was at his wits end, regretting his decision of taking the two of them together. He was already thinking of doubling the fare. All of a sudden, everything happened so fast that one could not fathom the whole gravity of the situation.

All Binodini heard was sound of hooves…. a crash….a bang and the loud screaming of a man in pain. She saw her husband getting down from the rickshaw and running to the aid of an overturned horse-drawn buggy.

What really happened was that the small buggy was being pulled by four of the best horses that one had ever seen before; the speed was unmanageable even though the driver of the buggy did try to reign in the horses to prevent the accident with the cycle rickshaw. The result was of course what happened … at this time of the afternoon, the streets wore a bare look and Beral Babu was the only living organism present due to his sweet expedition.

Leaving his wife to balance the many packages from her precarious seat atop the cycle rickshaw, he went to help.

The buggy lay overturned on its sides, its wheels turning madly in the air. Beral Babu managed to pull out the driver of the buggy from under one of the horses. The tall thin heavy-moustached man seemed quite alive. Beral Babu helped in calming down the horses though from a safe distance. The driver, with Beral Babu's aid, tried to straighten the buggy but failing to do so, Beral Babu shouted at the rickshawala who from afar was watching with the interest of a curious bystander and trying to catch his lost breathe.

"Don't just stand there like a donkey, you ass! Come and help us."

The three together managed to pull out a tall aristocratic gentleman from under the overturned buggy. Other than a small gash on his temple, he seemed to be in one piece. He thanked the three for their effort; even made an attempt to smile bleakly at Binodini who was perched precariously at forty odd degree, trying to acknowledge the watery smile. She nodded her head vigorously; in doing so, her aanchol slipped low. She was in her own dilemma whether to save her husband's precious packages or keep her face covered.

The gentleman was quiet disoriented, groggy.... unable to stand tall without help; he was broad-shouldered, with a majestic moustache. The most striking feature was his shiny bald head... not a single strand in sight, just like an overturned boiled egg .

The gash on his temple, which was now bleeding quite heavily, seemed it would need stitches.

Beral Babu at once offered assistance. "Please come to my house and sit for a while...I will seek Suchitra's husband's help, though a vet by profession. He is sort of our family doctor, and he can stitch up the cut. It seems a little ugly now." Beral Babu's offer was made kindly and it was taken up quite graciously.

Long after the vet had left after administering a few required medical procedures, the gentleman relaxed for a while registering the kind graciousness of the couple.

He watched the woman of the house fanning him with a hand fan, and the man of the house pressing and rubbing his hands and feet as if trying to take the pain away.

Much later, the gentleman got up. "I have to take your leave; I feel much better now. I am grateful to you both for the kindness shown."

Beral Babu turned a slight light pink and shook his heavy matted head. "It was no big deal; we are used to doing this." It seemed as if he did this kind of graciousness on a daily basis.

The gentleman slowly made his way out; just as he was about to climb into the buggy, which though bruised, was quite road worthy, he suddenly turned and laid a hand on Beral Babu's shoulder. Pressing gently, he said, "It will be of great pleasure to me and my wife if we can ever return this favour of yours. Don't hesitate to ask." Hearing this, Beral Babu turned a herring red, somehow trying to nod in acknowledgement.

The gentleman continued, "For now, you both join us for a high tea on the 16th of this month…it will be our pleasure; so, please do not refuse."

The buggy sped away leaving behind a thick cloud of dust.

"Horses are so dangerous and I would never sit on one even if it was for free," said Beral Babu.

His wife seemed lost in her own thoughts not paying much attention; this gentleman was so different, not from their part of the world, he was so articulate, and artful in his way of carriage….roused a sense of curiosity in her to know more.

"I hope we will be going over," she said. Beral Babu, who was still rambling about the dangerous side of horses, was a little taken aback. "Going where?"….Binodini smiled seeing her husband's lost look; she added more confusion to his misery, "I would like to sit on one."

Beral babu asked with a full steam of curious misery, "Sit on What?"

Flinging a naughty smile at her husband, she went inside to clear the living room, and bring it back to its old tidy self.

For a few days after this incident, Binodini's thoughts dwelled on the gentleman over and over again; his crisp silk dhuti and punjabi with gold buttons that had a twinkle of white fire in it, his fine black shoes polished to a mirror…this daydreaming of his wife was not missed by Beral Babu either. Often during the evenings, when the couple sat down in the companionship of a cup of tea, Binodini would sink into a gentle brooding silence, as if lost in an ocean of thoughts.

It was just another of those slow moving days of the week; Binodini was tucking in the mosquito net, Beral Babu sat on one of the chairs with a glass of warm milk in his hand trying to blow away the cream that had accumulated on the surface when suddenly she said, "Is it the sixteenth of the month yet?"

He looked at her long and steady, and answered very deliberately, "It is already the twenty fifth of the month, just five more days to completion."

Binodini looked at her husband a little thoughtfully biting on her lower lip pensively as she left the room.

Beral Babu did follow his wife's present preoccupation, what bewildered him was her behaviour. She never ever earlier had shown such interest in a total stranger, he wandered and kept thinking.

It was just one of those days; Beral Babu was at the office and Binodini was sweeping the front cobblestone pathway of her home when suddenly she heard the approaching hooves of a buggy.

A tall liveried driver got down and made a clank, clank sound with the latch of the gate. Binodini's heart did a nervous somersault; she quickly straightened her sari and went up to the man. He saluted very smartly and handed her a sleek white envelope. The envelope's whiteness was a sharp contrast to the honey warm complexion of her hands. A very manly, yet soft perfume was emanating from it, something sleek and suave. Her heart beat a little faster just like the beat of African drums; she sank down on weak knees on the steps leading up to the verandah.

A sense of curiosity and excitement was slowly rising at the pit of her stomach. She opened the envelope tenderly and slipped out the card gently. The writing was neat and precise but for illiterate Binodini it was all black.

English was Greek to her. She could just about read Bangla. All said and done, she was dying to know what was written on the card.

She could not concentrate on any of her household chores and waiting for her husband who would come home only in the evening would surely and slowly kill her.

She straightened her hair with her fingers and drawing her aanchol over her head, she decided to go over to Suchitra's house. An educated and erudite woman who was a twelfth pass from a government school, surely, she could read a bit of what was written.

Suchitra lived very near to Binodini's house; she was a few years older than Binodini and since she was from Haldia, a port town of Kolkata, she was smarter than the likes of Binodini. She lived with her widowed mother-in-law, an old woman in her sixties, hawk-eyed and beak-nosed; she hardly ever had any kind words to say to anyone.

Seeing Binodini walk into the house at that time of the morning, she started off, "You have come to meet our Suchitra; don't you know she has a lot of work to do unlike you….nowadays youngsters are so lazy……I used to cook for twenty people and never once…." continued the old woman. Luckily, Binodini saw her friend signaling to her from the kitchen; getting an opening, she slipped past the old woman.

In the warmth of the small kitchen, the two friends sat close together on low wooden stools. Suchitra handed her friend a cup of steaming hot tea sweetened with a lump of jaggery accompanied with a plate of gujiyas. "Made them just yesterday… taste and see."

Binodini was too excited to eat anything; keeping her hardly touched cup to one side, she handed over the envelope into Suchitra's curious hands. "Read and tell me what is written."

Her friend looked very surprised and as she drew out the card from inside, a gasp left her lips. "Who gave you this…..must be the wrong address?" For some time after that, Suchitra's lips moved silently reading the contents of the card.

Binodini could now hardly contain her curiosity. "Tell me also what is written," almost shaking her friend's arm. Her friend indicated for her to wait; after all, it was all in English and would take her a little while.

"First tell me how you came about this invitation? Do you know the Raibahadurs? They are the one and only royal family of India who are not only rich beyond imagination but also related to the queen herself." Suchitra spoke very slowly and deliberately as if speaking to a dimwit, waiting for her words to sink in.

After having heard all that Binodini had to say, she said quite unpleasantly, "It was your lucky day that he chose to crash his royal carriage in front of you....you have been invited to the palace for high tea. The Raibhadur seems to have penned down the invitation with his own hands....a very exclusive invite I should say."

Suchitra, though quiet a decent soul, yet, all men are mortal and all women Eve's daughter, kept wandering how such people as the Beral's, who were just next to nobody, could get invited to such exalted circles.

As Binodini was about to leave, Suchitra said, "You are going to move in exalted circles now, eh! Binoo, do not forget us, especially small people like us."

Binodini felt hurt hearing these nasty words, seemed she had lost a friend that day, but her initial hurt was soon overcome by the exciting thought of the invite. No work got done that day; she hardly did any cooking, and waiting for her husband to get home was the longest.

On that day of all days as it usually happens...in all tense and exciting situations, all the buses were on strike, and the few trams plying on the roads were slow and filled to the brim with human life struggling to get home after a long day's hard toil in the offices. Beral Babu hated congestion and suffered from severe claustrophobia of enclosed spaces. He and Badai da had walked up to the city square before they managed to catch hold of a cycle rickshaw.

The fellow was such a slow poke; he took his own sweet time stopping from time to time to catch his breath, insinuating that he would charge for three people. Badai da, who was laughing his head off, added more insult to injury while they were paying the fare. "Now, now, Beral Babu, he did pull all that weight, didn't he? He deserves a little extra from you."

Even before he could raise the latch of the gate, Binodini was out on the cobblestone pathway with a wide grin on her face; she seemed terribly excited but Beral Babu was too exhausted from his ordeal to even think....why she was so excited?

"Wash yourself and change quickly; I have something to show you," she said to him.

Beral Babu gulped more than two odd glasses of cold water and much, much later, as he sat down the empty cup on the side table, he took the eagerly proffered envelope from his wife's hands.

He gingerly read his name in a crisp and neat hand, and then read the invite but unlike his wife, he felt no excitement or joy... rather a mixture of apprehensions and nervousness hit him.

"The invitation is for the seventh of next month; we may not go after all. Their world is so different from ours.... he has invited us but I am sure he does not really expect us to go...." Seeing Binodini's expression, he trailed off to a lame silence.

Looking into her large eyes, he saw the excitement he had not seen in many a years; she had then come as a young bride all of just fourteen. She just had not heard what her husband had said. Her soft cheeks had spots of pink, and she was lost in her own thoughts.

"It is a very exclusive address, and Suchitra was saying they are very, very royal."

Beral Babu exclaimed! "What! You have shown this to your friend? Could you not wait for me to come home? She and her husband are such parrots! Soon the whole neighbourhood will come to know, we may not go after all!"

All good words lost upon busy minds....... "Why will we not go? After all we have been invited, I wander if their home is like a palace, the zamindar's house in my village was so big, must be bigger than that I suppose."

Beral Babu smiled at his wife's innocent words. Undecided, they turned in for the night.

Sleep did not come easy to Binodini; seventh of the next month was not very far off... just ten odd days in hand to make all the preparations. She would discuss with her friends tomorrow what to wear...jewellery to put on, hairstyle to be done. Then a little doubtfully, she thought of her sparse wardrobe.......anyway choices have to be made.......

While Beral Babu's rhythmic snoring hit the peaceful walls of the room, Binodini was tossing, turning, wandering, planning, and thinking. In her excitement, she even forgot to lock the front door, tied the mosquito net twice inside out and even left the milk on the stove that was still very hot from the glowing embers....the milk boiled over and over again turning into a solid burnt mass.

Next day was uneventful; Beral Babu left for office, letting her know he might be late in case the bus strike continued. There was lightness in her steps as she hummed and did her chores.

On the other hand, Beral Babu could not work at all; his preoccupation did not let him even enjoy the lovely meal that Binodini had packed for him.... anyway.... his loss, another's gain. He looked at the stringy stray that lived in the office compound. What a simple and peaceful life he had; no such interruptions other than when Salaam khan's bamboo cane fell on his back for entering the lunch hall.

Lunch over, Beral Babu was back at his corner. The postman had just left him with another piece of news to digest... they say when it rains it pours, and pouring it was.

Debendra Ghosh, the office 'bard' as he was called by the others due his charming capacity of being extremely nosy and making everyone's personal life public, today of all days decided to shower all his good intentions on Beral Babu. According to Ghosh, he was a poor fat slob who really needed his help.

Leaning over conspiratorially over the old wooden office table and sticking his mischievous face into his victims, he said with a whisper of secrecy, "Ki Beral Babu, you seem quiet disturbed, I have been watching you all day; you did not even finish your tiffin…Haricharan's lucky day today I suppose."

Ghosh lowered himself down on one of the rickety wooden chairs, taking out a small silver box from the pocket of his punjabi. He took out a pan and stuffed it into his wide mouth, "Betel chewing makes the brain run faster, have you thought about my offer yet?" Seeing Beral Babu's bewildered look, he shook his head sympathetically, "Coming to Puri with us?"

Beral Babu had forgotten all about it; hence, he just shook his matted head. His present dilemma was to Ghosh's advantage, he who thrived on juicy tales. Further encouragement broke down Beral Babu and he unloaded his whole heart to Ghosh.

Ghosh swallowed a whole lot of saliva; then thought something and said, "Do you have any idea who Raibhadur is? Do you have any idea to where you have been invited to….I would have given my head to the butcher for such an invitation."

Ghosh's parting remark kept ringing in his ears. All said and done, the office bard did his work…. soon the whole office knew about it.

Wherever he went, be it for a nature call or a visit to the tearoom, everyone who would be talking would but fall silent the moment they saw him. Between eight in the morning till the time he spoke to Ghosh, the equation of his stature had changed in everyone's eyes. Even Salaam khan's salute had more stiffness and crispness to it. For a change, even Badai da refrained from any of his staple sarcasm. Journey back home was hectic; yet, without any marked unpleasant comments from Badai da.

Much later, while having dinner, Beral Babu mentioned about the letter from his aunt.... she is planning to stay for a while. Binodini digested the news with silence.

A day odd later, Beral Babu reached home to find the front gate and the main door wide open, very unlike Binodini. He hurried inside the house wandering as to.......

Loud high-pitched voice greeted him; Rangamashi had arrived. She had come from the station on her own; that meant expenditure of an unwanted kind. This displeased her extremely and she was making it obvious to Binodini. Poor girl stood there with her head bent low as the old woman rattled on.

Rangamashi was not a woman of very pleasant disposition...in fact, she was short, squat, dark-skinned woman with a head full of dark grey matted hair that no amount of oil would ever settle down. She seemed to be in her sixties but vagaries of nature bellied her actual age of being just in her late forties.

Pan-stained lips broke into a wide smile that revealed a few missing incisors and canines. Standing up from the single bed that she was sitting on, she straightened her white sari that had seen better days.

As Beral Babu touched her feet, she gave her usual blessing, "May you have a hundred sons," gloating in her own mind that at least she still had full control and command over this nephew of hers who was still such a simpleton and fell for all her schemes and wiles. Sad her sons kept her at a distance.... their wives were extremely cunning and saw through all her plans and manipulations.... someday.... all that would change.

This time, she had come with the intention of staying for a longer period.... last time her foolish nephew had booked the tickets early. With her sister passing away, that position of an elder had fallen vacant....which she could easily fill up.... would need a little cleverness and cunningness on her part.

Might be she could persuade her twice-displaced niece to visit....

men are but men even foolish ones like her nephew....need to sow their wild oats for the continuation of the species.

Her twice displaced niece was still unmarried even though she was a few years older than Beral Babu....all marriage proposals for her had fallen through.... one look at her head of matted hair and her large buck tooth, boys seemed to abhor the very idea of marriage.

4. Rangamashi's Five Days

Rangamashi's thoughts were running like the hounds after a hare; her niece Nooti would in fact do splendidly....help sow his wild oats, and of course, hand over the house keys to her but as for Binodini, one needed her too. The girl was an amazing cook and one needed someone to do all the work; so, a compromise would have to be done but that was for later...now....

As Rangamashi sat on the bed, she kept having these wild and terrible thoughts. Binodini studied the old woman feeling angry yet sorry for her. Her husband had told her all.... how her sons do not take care of her.... the poor woman stayed in one of the rooms of the large house built by her husband who had been a homeopathy doctor. Anyway, she was responsible to some extent for her own state.... troubling her daughters in law.... quarrelling over petty matters made her very unpalatable.

She was old, and Binodini being the gentle and kind-hearted soul that she was, took all in her stride with a smile.

She hurried to the kitchen thinking about the number of chores that she had to finish which included washing the large number of dirty old saris that Rangamashi had especially handed to her while unpacking....

Finicky old woman, she had her own quirks and charms. A woman having more quirks, and no charms at all.

She just had one belief in life—to criticise and make others miserable; for now the sight of her favourite nephew pleased her the most, it was really very, very unfortunate that her dead sister did not listen to her and got him married to her twice-displaced niece. By now, the house would be full of nephews and nieces. She also could have visited more frequently.... even stayed on.

She did not like Binodini at all; according to her, the girl was like a cow with no mind of her own. Beral's wife should have been a more spirited creature, of course someone like her twice-displaced niece.

Every day was a battle for Binodini. It was full of trials for her and of course triumphs for the old woman. The harder she tried to please the old woman, the more she got criticised and more were the number of complaints for Beral Babu's ears when he returned home in the evenings.

Till her nephew's arrival in the evening, she would walk around strong, even go over to Suchitra's house to chat with her mother-in-law; of course, there would be more criticism and complaints but the moment she would hear her nephew at gate, she would start grumbling loudly holding her knee and rubbing her back.

Over evening tea, she would make sure her nephew came to know how cold the morning tea was or how hard the naro biscuits were, bouma was really after the few teeth she had left.

How everything back at her village was so nice and better tasting. Beral Babu would hear out the old woman with a patient ear chiding Binodini gently to be more careful in future.

A sweet soul that she was, she never once showed how hurt she felt, taking it all with a smile.

Suchitra did get over her usual jealousy; one day, she dropped by and told Binodini, "What are you doing the whole day? We do not even see you outside nowadays, what a lot of cooking you have done...Is it all meant for the visiting well?"

With no response from Binodini, Suchitra continued, "Believe me, just yesterday she was trying to tell my old woman about how she had not had anything to eat since morning."

Invariably, during evening tea, Rangamashi would drop hints about how busy she had been the whole day. Beral Babu would chide his wife in privacy and say, "Do not let the old woman do any work; after all she is our guest." For the rest of the evening, Binodini would be quite upset; Beral Babu would feel sad but he did not want to make his aunt unhappy.

Dinner time would put another big strain on their already strained relationship, and Rangamashi was never satisfied with anything whatsoever. She would eat all that was laid out in front of her; in fact, ask for more but as she would get up to wash her hands in the courtyard, she would start finding numerous faults with the food that she had just eaten. A little more salt in the dal, the fish needed a little more frying, the rice was a little raw....

Such was the list of endless good advices. It was a Sunday, another weekend; Beral Babu's favourite day of the week.

Binodini had got up earlier than usual for she wanted to make something special for all. After a bath, she attended to all her chores quickly, and then, as the orange ball rose in the eastern sky, she watered the Tulsi and uttered a silent prayer for all.

The dough made out of flour was kneaded to a perfection; dipped in ghee, it was ready to be rolled out into small luchis (a Bengali delicacy). On the other side, hot spicy potato curry was slowly simmering in the dying embers of the log, which she had flavoured with a gentle hand of curry leaves and dry red chilies. A cup of hot steaming tea in hand, she made her way to the bedroom.

Seeing the empty bed and open bathroom door, she wondered where her husband had gone so early in the morning.

As she was making her way back to the kitchen, she heard muted voices coming from the old woman's room, "So many years into your marriage....the house is so empty."

She did not want to hear the rest; she knew exactly what was being said. Leaving the cup on the cabinet near the door, with tears flooding her eyes, she made her way to the stone bench in one corner of the garden. She must have been sitting there for some time now when a voice behind her shook her from her silence "Binoo, why are you sitting here all alone? I was looking for you all over the house."

He stopped short in seeing her tear-stained face. Both sat in silent companionship; he took her soft hands in his and said, "I do not care what the world says…as far as she is concerned….you already know all about her state as it is, back in her village…."

"In my eyes, you are much above all this…my world revolves around you and you only." Binodini wiped her tears, slipped her soft fingers into his and smiled.

It was much later over breakfast that Beral Babu asked his aunt if she would like to do a little sightseeing; the offer was taken up graciously. Bus was out of question as Beral feared it would be jam-packed with struggling humanity; hence, cycle rickshaw was a better option. For a change, the old woman behaved well. The whole of Sunday was spent happily. Binodini tried to forget her initial sadness, and put in an extra effort to enjoy this rare treat.

"How much for these shingaras?" asked Rangamashi haughtily. The mithaiwala, a short potbellied man quite adept at selling his wares, answered back in the same tone, "Fifteen paisa a piece and hot at that, full of spicy potatoes and roasted peanuts."

In his many, many years of experience with man's gentler half, one supposes he must have never come across the likes of Rangamashi. Today, of all days, he had rubbed a very wrong person the very wrong way. He soon was subjected to a long lecture on how shingaras should be made, the shingaras back in her village were much larger filled with more filling and of course tastier—her voice was extremely loud and quiet offensive; the mithaiwala was no less either.

Soon, a small crowd of interested bypassers gathered. It was very embarrassing for Beral Babu as he would never dream of drawing such attention ever.

Sans the shingaras as the mithaiwala would not sell them any, in fact he too in a very loud and insulting manner asked the old woman to go back to her village and eat some there. After this cherry on the cake moment, they quietly made their way back home.

Rangamashi got up with a severe attack of gas and indigestion in the evening; all the chaat, pyaazi, and mishti were showing their true colours. After her seventh cup of tea and fifth visit to the 'kings' throne, she desperately requested her nephew for a doctor, as any further delay would kill her for sure. She burped, hiccupped and groaned loudly, passing foul smelling gas every now and then. Beral Babu was quite worried at the whole scenario. At this time of the night, getting a doctor was difficult and there was none at present in their residential colony, fees charged for a house call were so exorbitant.

Suchitra's husband was of course there even though a vet by profession. He was quite adept at dealing with all kinds of minor emergencies.

Doctor Radheshyam Gosain was a fine person, a real charmer with his clever words. He was tall, and fair complexioned; his egg-shaped head had a sparse growth of fine curly hair. All these complimented a short Hitler moustache. He had very shifty hands with fine narrow fingers that he kept clasping and unclasping. According to some, he had been bitten by a cow during its calf delivery, and had developed this nervous condition.

Most knew his secret desire to do MBBS but unfortunately, due to various constraints, he had ended up as a vet.

In his heart, he cherished the very idea of people calling him over for a medical advice; he was more than willing to please, and no fees charged whatsoever. Beral Babu rushed over to Suchitra's house.

The vet was at home; he was extremely pleased knowing that Beral Babu had come to him for medical consultancy.

He sincerely heard the serious nature of Rangamashi's medical condition; there was a look of very serious contemplation on his face. Then he picked up two bottles from the wooden cupboard in his consultancy room—one held a misty green liquid the other contained a pink liquid that foamed lightly when the bottle was shaken.

The stethoscope that swung from his neck was a bit large and on the heavier side—mostly meant for bigger animals.

The vet carefully checked the old woman's pulses and heartbeat. "Do not worry; her heart is in fine condition… so are her lungs, as for the other ailment, I shall give her medicine and she will be fine and fit as a fiddle in no time," said the vet all the while speaking only to Beral Babu. He was so used to speaking only to the owners of the animals he treated! Rangamashi felt extremely offended at being treated like a third person but thankfully her weak condition left her too listless to argue.

Asking for a tablespoon, he poured the misty green liquid into it and then he forced the old woman to gulp it down in one go; this was immediately followed by two tablespoon of the pink liquid.

Rangamashi's face first turned ashen, and then turned completely white; she somehow croaked, "Tch! Tch! Horrible …..I will die for sure if I drink this anymore; it smells of cow piss."

Seeing Beral Babu's worried look, the vet laid a calming hand on his shoulder and said, "Do not worry so my friend, it is my patented medicine, something I myself concocted way back in my veterinary college. It was very much appreciated by my then professor Major Dyer who used it in the army very prolifically. Just remember to give her a four-hourly dose, and no solid food for the next twenty four hours." The vet made his way out refusing a cup of tea from Binodini.

A very worried Beral Babu followed by Binodini saw him out; one could hear the loud groans and grunts of the old woman coming from inside the house, "She will recover I hope?" Beral Babu asked the vet very nervously.

"Aree…moshai, what are you worried about? She is safe. This same medicine cured Rakhal's Hira of gas and indigestion. The bloody cow had eaten something off the rubbish heap and was fouling the air like a steam engine!"

Binodini could hear no more; her peals of laughter could be heard till the end of the street.

Every four-hourly, both would get up to administer the medicines to Rangamashi, who after many protests would gulp them down. Binodini always had a small piece of jaggery to soothe down the taste of the medicine.

Slowly but surely the medicines worked, and soon, the old woman was out of bed.

It was that time of the morning when Binodini had many chores to do. Since Rangamashi's illness, cooking had come down to a simple boiled fare. "I am much better now bouma, and I cannot eat this food. Even animals will not touch this. I am going for a bath; when I return I want a proper meal, or I will tell Beral that you are trying to starve me."

Binodini's advice to have boiled food for the next few days drew the old woman's wrath, her face turned red like the mid-day sun.

"What? How dare you question my wishes? You do not want me to eat decently even in my own nephew's house…..I knew you had it in you to be so mean, it is a good thing my sister died when she did, at least she did not have to see these terrible days."

Binodini hurried to the kitchen to fulfill the old woman's wishes; she wanted peace in the house when her husband returned in the evening and to please the old woman further, she made a nice big bowl of payesh.

Small luchis with hot spicy potato curry was wolfed down without any hesitation by Rangamashi, followed by a large bowl of payesh.

"I shall not tell Beral anything but you mend your ways, learn to pay respect to elders," was the parting shot from her, leaving Binodini in the kitchen to finish her day's chores.

As she was sweeping the courtyard, the loud snoring emanating from inside the house hailed the arrival of a peaceful afternoon; uncontrollable giggles escaped her soft pink lips—truly…. a parody of affairs.

As she was settling her husband's clothes in his cupboard, a sleek white envelope fell out from its folds, leaving a trail of misty, suave and a very, very male fragrance in its trail. Binodini's heart missed a few beats and she felt a sense of curious nervous anticipation at the pit of her stomach, something she had not felt in many, many years now.

A sense of curious romance aroused in her; she walked up to the mirror, the afternoon sun was trailing in brightly lighting up the room, the figure in the mirror though sweetly plump but one could not have missed out the large doe-like eyes, soft and smooth honey complexion set to perfection by her very long thick black hair.

Wide arched eyebrows above a nice straight nose complimented with soft, pink wide lips, a lovely white smile and long arched neck attenuated by a thick gold chain. She raised her long artistic fingers and touched her soft pink cheeks.

Somewhere, somehow life had come to a standstill…like a still pool of stagnant water.

Rangamashi was leaving the next day; afterwards, she would broach the topic…..

That evening, Beral Babu was a little late as he had gone to the market to pick up a few gifts for Rangamashi. Making choices for her was no easy matter; anyway, every time she had visited them, a sari or pan masalas and mishtis were the expected and liked gifts.

Over tea, Rangamashi opened her gifts. "Nice cotton sari but the border could have been a little wider or it could have been a little whiter. Neko's nephew….of course you know him quite well, he was the fat boy with a bald patch on his head," she said.

Not bothered whether the others were interested in this kind of information, she continued…. "He used to have scabies, which he caught from the stray dog near his house. I remember, as kids, you both used to go skinny-dipping together in the village pond. See my big boy blushing." saying this, she crackled and laughed.

"Now he has a big shop in the village, his saris are so white, I always buy from him," she said.

Looking at Binodini with evident dislike, she kept on, "My eldest bouma, Surojit's wife, has so much regard and respect for me; she will take my consent every morning as to what to cook and what to do. She has given me three handsome grandsons and this pujo, she gave me fifty rupees in my hand for my sari; indeed, such a nice girl," said Rangamashi with sarcastic grin.

She, for a change, liked the small steel box in which to keep her pan and betel nuts, and the three types of fragrant masalas was also well taken. She was not the type to give up easily; so she continued with her next stage of the plan.

"From here, I will be going to Basanti's house in Hoogly…you know her… I had tried to fix up her daughter's marriage with you, very smart girl… still unmarried. She never agreed to marry anyone… I wonder why."

Dropping such subtle hints, she made her nephew extremely embarrassed and Binodini fumed in silence.

"After so many years, let such topics lie low," Beral Babu managed to say.

5. Dropping a Bomb

Just as they were finishing their second cup of tea and Rangamashi was stuffing herself with the remaining malpuas, there was a loud knock on the main door.

Beral Babu wondered aloud as to who could have come at this odd hour. It was none other than the office bard. He invited the pan chewing Debendra Ghosh into the house as he was making a silly attempt to smile with his stained and broken teeth.

"You must be Beral Babu's aunt; it's my great honour to have met you before you leave," Ghosh said while touching the old woman's feet with a great show of respect. Rangamashi loved feeling important and being the centre of attraction. Ghosh was a clever and astute man, and soon, wormed his way into the old woman's affections. Propping himself with much familiarity next to her on the bed he soon struck up small talk.

Binodini made some more tea and brought in some eatables for the guest. Ghosh got up and bent low in a very comical manner to take the cup from her, as he chewed on a piece of spicy savoury, Binodini's eyes fell on his ears, each had a conical tip and were covered on the edges with thick bushy spiky hair. She somehow stifled a giggle drawing a warning look from the old woman. Long ago, as a little girl back in her village, she had once seen a bat with such ears hanging upside down from a mango tree.

"Nice boudi…. you must have made them, in the office in fact we all love Beral Babu's tiffin….you are such an excellent cook, I will ask my wife to come and learn from you," said he in between mouthfuls.

Rangamashi did not at all like this shift of attention from her to Binodini. "It seems you do not know, whatever she has learnt is from me….I was famed in my village for my cooking, people would even lick their plates and fingers clean." Beral Babu gave a conspiratorial smile at Binodini as if trying to tell her I know the truth.

"Anyway, I have to leave now.... Beral Babu, my Puri offer still stands.... you have not given any thought to it I suppose," said Ghosh.

Rangamashi could not contain her delight at hearing this, "If you all are going, then I would also love to come; it is a long wish of mine to see lord Jagannath."

Ghosh had a big smirk on his face as if he was going to share the greatest secret ever known to mankind. "I am so sorry for you mashima but this desire of yours will remain unfulfilled, as they have a much more important event to attend. Your nephew is now moving in such exalted circles, real royalty I should say where drinking, smoking, and dancing is as normal as breathing."

Ghosh continued adding his own spicy bits and pieces; Rangamashi's face was livid with rage, the very thought of her not being able to go to Puri just because of some invitation to some royal palace made her angry.

Indeed, how can a village simpleton like her nephew get such an invitation, whereas her sons who were no less educated got no such offer. This very thought made her furious and wild with rage.

She lashed out at innocent Binodini. "It is all because of this girl, she puts such ideas into my nephew's head, now for all you know we will soon hear of smoking and drinking in this house of my dead sister."

All fell silent; Ghosh beat a hurried departure, the old woman fumed even after her nephew tried to pacify her saying they were not going at all and it was just an invitation. Binodini went to her bedroom and closed the door...there were no more tears to be shed. Every ordeal in life reaches a peak where it can hurt no more.

Next morning, the situation was no better. Rangamashi's behaviour was extremely offensive driving Binodini to tears; even the packed lunch of sweets and spicy savouries were not able to calm down the heated atmosphere. Beral Babu had taken a day off from the office to see Rangamashi off, a good man at heart, yet, he did not at all like his aunt's behaviour with his wife.

Binodini bent down to touch Rangamashi's feet to take her blessing but the old woman moved away sharply, turning away her face.

Beckoning to her nephew, she said in a very loud and dictatorial voice, "We are pundits and we treasure our culture and traditions; if you listen to this girl, you will bring bad name to all of us... let me know if you decide to go to Puri."

Something snapped within Beral Babu, a man known for his goodness and patience. "You are a guest in my house; so, I will request you to maintain your limits. By insulting my wife, you are insulting me too.... what we do is our personal matter, please refrain yourself."

Binodini had neither seen her husband look so angry before nor had she ever heard him speak in such manner.

Today, first time in so many years of her marriage, he had stood up for her, sharing her humiliation and sorrow. Tears of joy filled her eyes; the cycle rickshaw had long left, leaving behind a sense of security and oneness between the two of them that was never there earlier.

She looked at her husband....a good man at heart...what their life had come to....would she never be able to fill the empty void that existed?

In so many years of their marriage, this camaraderie and oneness had been missing, she had come as a young bride of fourteen, her mother-in-law, though a kindly woman, never spared her of unkind words when a mistake happened; her father-in-law though a good man, never said a word against his wife, though would sometimes bestow silent sympathetic looks on Binodini.

Her husband too had maintained silent neutrality, too afraid to say anything. On such occasions, she always had felt very angry with him. After the old people had passed away, life had assumed smaller nuclear proportions with minor disruptions here and there but otherwise smooth.

As the truth runs, for a chrysalis to turn into a butterfly it has to face the fire of hell; it is a true warrior that emerges a champion overcoming all obstacles and tests of life.

Beral Babu wiped away her tears, smiled and said, "You have always been the only shade in my life, taking everything with a smile, I am there for you; come stop crying and make me a nice cup of tea."

Dark clouds replaced with a bright sunny smile; both made their way into the house, hand in hand.

Life held a different meaning after that; early morning as Beral Babu got ready for the office, he hummed under his breath. It had been a long time since his early college days that anyone had ever heard him sing or even hum.

Just as he closed the latch of the front iron gate, he turned and said to her, "Check out what we both can wear for the tea party; we are going.... after all, one does not get such invitations every day." He smiled very wickedly knowing that was what she wanted to hear him say.

Binodini hurried through her chores; life had become quite exciting and sweet.

Soon a little while after mid-day, both Suchitra and Sunanda came over followed by Tara; the pile of red-bordered white saris left them confused and scratching their heads in vain. The whole lot looked so drab, all permutations and combinations were discussed between the very whites, whites and the cremes but ultimately, there was no success whatsoever.

The only silk sari she had, had seen better days. It was too late to get a blouse stitched now; the few blouses that she had were all white in colour. Tara was the only one with a lot of imagination. She had some handmade lace back home, which she was sure would improve the overall look if put around the neck and the sleeves. Offering to do the needful herself, she took the blouse home.

Her friends left late in the afternoon but not before having nice hot cups of masala-flavoured tea and piping-hot cauliflower pakoras with spicy green chutney made out of garden fresh green chilies and freshly plucked coriander leaves.

Beral Babu had an uneventful day at the office; the only time there were some ripples on the smooth surface of the lake was when Debendra Ghosh tried to strike up another episode like the one at his home a day or two earlier. Unlike his nature, Beral Babu snapped at Ghosh, and asked him to firmly to stay within his limits.

Everyone at the office were a little taken aback at this new aggressive Beral Babu of theirs; for the rest of the day, everyone took extreme care not to displease Beral Babu in anyway.

He reached home to find Binodini waiting for him with a big wide smile. Dinner was a quiet and simple affair; on his insistence, Binodini broke her habit of many, many years of eating only after her husband would finish his. The loving couple laughed and joked about the day's happenings over their meal.

It was while in bed that Beral Babu asked, "What have you decided to wear? Why don't you wear the sari that I have bought for you for this pujo or you can wear the one I bought for you last year."

Binodini turned to her husband and said in a very quiet voice, "What difference does it make? They all look the same."

The next day saw a flurry of activities in the 'Beral' household. Dhuti and saris to be cleaned and ironed…. her friends turned up to help her out…. it was decided that she would wear her hair in a long braid for that suited her the most; as for the jewellery, she possessed only a few pieces. Hence, not much of a choice there…. small delicate tops for her ears and the red white bangles teamed with two thin gold bangles for her wrists, the chains that she usually wore were cleaned with toothpowder to give them a shine.

Tara worked her magic on the old blouse; it really looked pretty.

That evening, Beral Babu was late in coming home; he slipped two large packages of brown paper bags into Binodini's surprised hands, humming a soft tune as he washed and changed, her loud cry of delight was all that he was waiting to hear.

He saw her face break into a lovely smile as she held up the light blue silk sari against her and looked into the long mirror of the old dressing table; the other bag contained brown belles of soft suede, and the shoes fitted her small feet beautifully.

Smiling indulgently, he said, "Won't my beautiful wife give me a cup of tea today?"

Biting her lips at the corner and exclaiming out aloud at her forgetfulness, she hurried into the kitchen.

Beral Babu sat back in his favourite armchair, a satisfied and pleasurable smile playing on his lips. When Binodini had come as young bride of fourteen…..and he had just appeared for his B. Com exam…no job meant no money, his mother always took the decision for everything.

When his father passed away, he was already in a comfortable job at the bank… his mother did not move to the village but continued staying with them…he did not want to hurt her feelings and she continued making the decisions.

Somewhere, somehow he forgot all about his Binodini…all he did was to do what others wanted him to do….he became a good son…a dutiful nephew…. a failed husband…he never ever bothered to find out what she liked…his mother had always insisted on these drab white saris….in so many years, he had never ever thought about her likes or dislikes.

As she made the tea, her hands were shaking; she was so lost in her thoughts that she added salt to the tea instead of sugar.

She dropped the plate of biscuits and almost toppled over the large saucepan full of milk. Her husband, on seeing the delay, came to the small kitchen lit dimly by a small overhead bulb. Pulling a small wooden stool, he sat near his wife.

She passed him the cup; as he sipped the salty tea, he realised her folly and with a wide smile, he said, "People living in the mountains take salty tea; it not only cuts down on sugar but is also extremely healthy."

Seeing her blushing, he continued, "Today even the biscuits have a soft earthy flavour and an extra crunch… really unique."

Binodini giggled and turned away trying to hide her embarrassment. One could hear the two laughing and enjoying their tea in that small kitchen.

6. High Tea a the Raibhadurs

It was almost three in the afternoon when the familiar sound of hooves was heard, followed by clank, clank of the latch of the small iron gate. Beral Babu, who was already ready and in the process of hailing a tonga for their journey, stopped short on the road. He came back and hurried inside to his wife who was getting ready.

"The Raibahadur has sent his own buggy to take us.... really a good man."

The fashionable buggy drawn by two of the most magnificent horses drew many onlookers; Binodini was helped up by the liveried driver. As she adjusted her blue silk sari, she made a lovely picture.... her blouse looked pretty, set apart by the delicate handmade lace. Beral Babu looked smart in a starched dhuti and punjabi, and nice black shoes matched up equally with black socks.

The buggy was extremely luxurious; black enamel painted body with brass handles on the single door, soft satin cushions in baby pink, foldable brass edged stairs, with high seats for the guard and the driver. The dun coloured horses soon put speed into their hooves, the large ostrich feathers that decorated their heads bobbed up and down as they trotted.

Raibahadur Sangram Singh's house was at the other end of the city.... in one of the most fashionable and well-appointed areas of Kolkata. The buggy speed across market places, parks.... gradually the stingy roads opened into broader well-paved roads, neat sidewalks, the houses were neat, large and well-appointed with lawns and lovely gardens. Horse drawn buggies and chauffeur driven cars could be seen on the roads.

One could catch glimpses of English memshahebs in their pretty hats being driven by liveried drivers. The neighbourhood was quiet unlike the hustle and bustle in their colony, where each neighbour was aware of the others' existence. Each time the carriage would slow down in front of any of the houses, Binodini's heart would skip a beat. The broad roads, now lined with tall trees on both sides, had fewer and fewer houses. Ultimately, there were no more houses… only lush green trees on both sides. At long last, the buggy stopped in front of tall iron gates with huge brass knobs; there were two large brass lions on either sides of the tall columns of the gate as if ready to spring upon any enemy that was to come.

The gate was opened by two uniformed guards who looked very smart in their blue tunics and white pants. Until now, not much could be seen due to the high walls that surrounded the palace grounds. Binodini could just about catch a glimpse of the palace through the tall trees in full red and orange bloom at this time of the year.

The buggy sped on, the majestic horses breathing white funnels of cloud as they galloped on the soft gravelled turf and gradually the tree-lined path gave away to extensive well-manicured lawns, potted palms, creeping philodendron, and frangipanis. There was a large duck pond with beautiful white swans. The palace had solid grey walls with covers of green moss spreading their passionate fingers into the tiny crevices and ridges. As they approached closer, the large bay windows with stained glass gave away hints of the party inside, and soft music played on the piano floated to her ears. The buggy slowed down as it approached the portico making a grand entry; two uniformed servants standing at the bottom of the marble stairs rushed to assist them.

As Binodini got down from the buggy, she breathed in the beauty and majesty of the palace. The majestic portico was supported by tall Grecian columns of white Markhana marble. They were ushered up the steps very respectfully, the large dark brown teak door was wide open, and standing at the head of the stairs was Raibahadur himself ready to welcome his two special guests.

"It is my great pleasure that you both have come... welcome madam to my home," he bowed in a very fashionable manner touching his chest with his broad manly hand. Binodini blushed and drew on her aanchol; Beral Babu folded his hands respectfully in front of this great humble king of a man, and offered the small gift of sweetmeat that he was carrying with great care. The Raibahadur thanked him profusely, and holding Beral Babu lovingly by the shoulders, took them both inside.

Binodini gasped aloud! She was so struck by the beauty of the large saloon that could have easily taken in more than a hundred odd guests. Today, there were about thirty very distinguished looking guests, among them some were British and others Indian... the very crème de la crème of Kolkata. The room had warm wooden panelled walls, deep red carpet in which her feet sank softly as she walked, the tall hand-painted ceilings of gild had motifs of roses, peacocks, and wild vines, the many large chandeliers that hung from the ceiling lit up the room brightly.

"Let me introduce to you all a very brave young man and his very gracious wife who saved my life; their humbleness and kindness has touched my heart like none other." Beral Babu could just about smile faintly; all this was just too much for him. As he got introduced, names lay heavy on his ears and quite a few titles and royalties among the guests. Binodini stood near her husband smiling and folding her hands respectfully as they were introduced.

Beral Babu had never ever touched anything stronger than tea his whole life; he refused the glass of red wine that was offered to him. The Raibahadur smiled at his hesitation and said, "I myself will make something special for both of you," beckoning them both to follow him to the bar at one corner of the room.

The bar was made out of mahogany colour wood with a glass top that housed an aquarium. Binodini squealed with delight at the sight of so many different types of fishes. The Raibahadur, seeing her peeping through the glass, said, "These flat silver colour fishes at this corner are called golden angels; they are very fierce by nature. I got them from Thailand on my last trip." Pointing to the other fishes, he said, "These are the ones I caught myself in the Ganges, and this loner is my all time favourite; it is a river catfish that feeds on smaller and weaker fishes but here in this tank, he is outnumbered; by nature he is very clever and cunning."

Binodini sipped her blue-coloured drink served in a small crystal goblet that caught the lights from the chandeliers above; it foamed lightly at the edges as she stirred it with a horsehead-shaped glass stirrer.

The men were talking and since she knew none of the women, her eyes wandered drinking in the beauty of the room. There was a large fireplace built out of black granite in front of which was a small neat pile of logs. What drew Binodini's attention was a large painting of a black horse; it looked so alive as if ready to leap out of the painting. There were many hunting trophies adorning the walls along with a large number of very old paintings. As she wandered a little, she strayed into the next room, which though not so large was as splendid as the saloon; it had a long dining table that was being readied for the feast by many a liveried servants.

What caught her attention was the wide staircase made out of deeply polished wood with thick brass railings that shown like gold. It was leading to the upper stories of the palace. Binodini had an overwhelming feeling of being watched and she looked up and her eyes caught the sight of a figure dressed in red and gold standing at the head of the stairs; it was but just a glimpse of a beautiful apparition like figure, looking down kindly and smiling at her.

"Aha.... there you are; come Binodini, if you permit me to call you so since you both are much younger to me, let me introduce you to my beautiful wife Lady Sreelata," said the Raibahadur. Hearing her name being called, Binodini turned round for a second but in the next moment, when she turned to look, the figure was gone.

Lady Sreelata was tall, fine-boned, and extremely gorgeous in a very exotic way. Her long black hair was like a curtain of silk that fell in a wave till her shoulders, she wore a single string of creamy pearls that glowed against her dusky skin, her pink sari was of the finest chiffon, and she wore a deep-necked sleeveless blouse of leaf green brocade. She held Binodini's face with her long delicate many-ringed fingers and blew her a loving kiss on her cheeks; Binodini was overwhelmed by this gesture. Her hostess left a trail of sweet heady perfume of flowers in her awake; tossing back her loose wave of hair, she said, "My husband has spoken so much about you both; I was waiting to meet you. His mother has taken the kids to Europe for a holiday, and I am all alone in this big house of mine; it becomes pretty lonely here."

Binodini's mind kept wondering about the woman she had seen standing at the head of the stairs but she was too hesitant to ask.

"Come Binodini, I will introduce you to some of my friends; they to want to meet you."

Taking her empty goblet, she asked the waiter to refill it. To her surprise, none of the women were haughty. In fact, they were very nice to her beyond her own expectations. She sat next to Lady Sreelata on the black chesterfield; the women carried out small talk and Binodini listened and learnt. She observed their way of carrying out conversations, their fine chiffon and silk saris.; expensive jewellery set with diamonds, pearls, rubies, and emeralds, and neatly tied chignons set apart with hairpins of gold and silver. Some did smoke slim cigarettes on holders, and others drank wine and brandy. The soft gentle-edged sophistication that these women possessed was missing in her part of the world.

All were invited to tea by the Raibahadur himself. After some time, Binodini moved with all the other guests to the dining hall; the servants had done a splendid job. The long table groaned under the wonderful layout of the finest cakes, pastries, wide variety of biscuits, mishtis and fruits, some of which she had never ever seen or tasted in her life.

"These mishtis remind me of my childhood days in my grandmother's house in Cuttack," said the Raibahadur who was relishing the ones that Beral Babu had got for him. "These just melt in the mouth," he spooned a mouthful into his wife's mouth asking her to taste.

"Binodini has made them for you," said Beral Babu.

"Then I should kiss her hands," said the Raibahadur laughing aloud seeing Binodini blushing a pretty pink.

Much later, they all sat down for tea; it was served in fine, delicate bone china cups, the hot liquid smelt of flowers, herbs, and spices.

After most of the guests had left, they were invited by the Raibahadurs to see the grounds of the palace; peacocks roamed the grounds freely. "You must come in the mornings to see them dance," said Lady Sreelata.

The kennels housed six of the most ferocious looking German shepherds. "They guard the palace grounds at night," informed one of the uniformed handlers of the dogs.

"Come both of you.... I shall show you my pride and my joy."

Saying this, the Raibahadur led them to his stables housing one of the finest majestic animals that one had ever seen. These are Hanoverians, a proud breed.... need gentle handling while riding; this is an Arabian mare ridden only by my wife, pointing out to a tall slim-legged horse that neighed and hoofed the ground as soon as she saw her mistress. There was just one old horse in the last stable. "This is the last generation of one the greatest war horses of my family; he is blind and almost more than twenty odd years old, the pair that pulled your buggy are thorough breeds, came with the British to India."

"Do you ride, Binodini?" asked Lady Sreelata. Binodini giggled and said, "As a small girl back in my village, I had once sat on a water buffalo; it was pretty uncomfortable I should say." Hearing this, all laughed aloud... loudest of all—Beral babu.

There never was a more mismatched relationship, but as the saying goes friendship often happens between the most unlikely. The Raibahadur put an arm around Beral Babu and the two walked together as if they had known each other for a very long, long time.

"The polo ponies of mine... I keep them at the turf club," said the Raibahadur. "We have matches almost every month; the Maharaja of Raipur and the Maharani are ardent players of the game. My luck has not been supporting me much nowadays. Have you ever watched a polo match?" he asked Binodini. Seeing her nodding, he smiled and said, "We have to rectify that, don't we?"

It was time for them to leave... it is said every fairytale has to come to an end but for **SOME, IT IS JUST A BEGINNING TO AN END.**

Binodini clung to every minute of her visit; their host and hostess saw them off, the horses picked up speed as they left the palace grounds. Buses honked loudly, trams chugged past, people hurrying, and of course, the mean and mad tongas of Kolkata were no different.

Binodini treasured all the maddening sweet memories of the day. It was almost half past eight in the evening when they reached home. Binodini hummed as she changed; this was the first time that Beral Babu heard his wife humming and he felt glad that they had gone. A large package was left by the guard on the side table; Binodini opened it to find that it was full of many delights from the evening's party.

Sleep was difficult to come; they both chatted long into the night. The next day, Beral Babu left for the office with tiffin full of exotic cakes, biscuits, and mishtis. Binodini put a little bit extra so that he could share with his friends. With no cooking to be done, she had a pleasant well laid-back day.

It was almost mid-day when her friends Tara, Sunanda, and

Suchitra came over to her place "How was it …? How did it go…?" Her friends eagerly sat next to her wanting to know every detail; Binodini narrated her evening's experiences while her friends listened wide-eyed. She offered them some cakes and biscuits along with piping hot masala flavoured tea. "What nice cakes… I love the one with oranges in it," said Tara. "I like the chocolate filled biscuits… they simply melt in the mouth," said Suchitra. "Oho…hum…I love them all," said Sunanda quickly stuffing the last piece of pineapple waffle into her mouth. They all laughed aloud, giggling like small girls, carefree and innocent.

Just a few days to the pujo and her friends had made their plans —Tara was going to her in-laws, whereas Suchitra was taking a trip to Darjeeling. Binodini knew her husband was more of a homebody; hence, she did not insist on going anywhere. The thought of visiting Rangamashi during the pujo was punishing by itself, as it was her husband was a little low on funds, bailing out poor relatives in dire straits.

Sunday saw a very busy Beral Babu as he had hired the contractor to carry out painting and denting work of the house. Majumdar was a sly and slimy chap from the borders, middle aged and quite round in the centre; he had a mouthful of unruly moustache and a large head full of shaggy grey hair, his short squat frame could be seen scurrying all over the place. The new very aggressive Beral Babu wanted work done his way and fast. For the hundredth time, Majumdar regretted in his mind for having taken up this job, that too on a Sunday. The Beral Babu of the old had been a laid back, lazy and sweet soul. He would have earned easy money but now that was not to be. "Majumdar, I am not going to pay anything today….you will come back tomorrow and complete this work first," shouted a very annoyed Beral Babu. A very cowed down and apologetic Majumdar stood before him promising to finish his work the next day.

"The house is very old and needs a lot of work to be done," said

Beral Babu as he fitted two extra bulbs in the kitchen so that his wife would not cut her finger while cutting vegetables as she usually did due to the dim light.

In the evening, as Beral Babu sat down with a nice cup of tea and the newspaper, the familiar sound of horse hooves was heard that stopped in front of the little gate. Soon, the sound of heavy boots was heard leading up to the front door. Beral Babu opened the main door on the first knock to find a tall uniformed heavy moustached buggy driver standing on the verandah. On seeing him, the fellow saluted smartly and handed him a small stiff white envelope. Opening it, Beral Babu turned and smiled at Binodini, "We have been invited to a polo match at the Kolkata turf club tomorrow; be ready by nine as the buggy will be coming to pick us up."

Binodini excitedly clapped her hands like a small child and said, "The Raibahadur never forgets his promise and it will be so exciting to see all those riders." Beral Babu smiled indulgently and said, "Wear the sari I gave you for the pujo, white always looks nice on a warm sunny morning." She gave a wide smile not having the heart to refuse to such a sweet request from her husband.

Their Grande' carriage arrived right on time the next morning, as she was getting into the buggy, Tara saw her leave. She rushed to tell Suchitra, "I suppose they have been invited again, so lucky I should say and Binodini looked so pretty and confident in red bordered white sari, even her hair looks different.... all tied up neatly. Both friends felt happy for her, yet, deep down there was little envy too as they both sat silently sipping tea and wandering.

They were the Raibahadur's guests and that meant the best seats in the house; they met some of the same crowd that they had met in the party, women dressed in sunny dresses or fine chiffon saris with low back sleeveless blouses, large floppy hats, and big sunglasses to protect them from the hot sun. As Binodini sat, a waiter arrived with a silver tray; on it were a lovely floppy hat in grey and two pairs of sunglasses. "My Lady has sent these for you both," he said. The match had already started, it was fierce.... both horses and riders trying to get the edge of each other. A frisky and sharp looking man sitting next to them adjusted his pince-nez on his blunt nose; he seemed to be quite a match freak. He introduced himself as 'Dash'... his knowledge was extensive.... he knew every rider and horse by name and he informed that even Lady Sreelata was also playing. According to him, the Raibahadur had very little chances of winning as two best of his players had fallen sick. Binodini did not like it a bit; she turned and said, "I wish for Raibahadur to win today no matter what."

In heavily accented Bengali, the gentleman exclaimed aloud, "Madam! Do not make such a wish; I have betted a lot of money on the Maharaja's team... if your wish is granted, I will be going home a very poor man."

As the battle became fiercer on the ground, the sun became stronger in the sky. Waiters served cooling sherbets and coconut water in tall crystal glasses, Binodini loved the ripe strawberries served with fresh cream.

Loud clapping and cheering hailed the winner; the Raibahadur had won and with Lady Sreelata by his side, he took the winner's trophy. They came to the VIP stand to greet their guests. With a tall glass of beer in hand, he came over to speak to Beral Babu, "I have won this match after five years, I feel great today my friend." Beral Babu congratulated and conveyed his happiness; just then a very unhappy and drunk Dash turned up, "I am finished, lost all my money, all because of madam here," said he pointing to Binodini with an accusing finger. A very bewildered Raibahadur looked at blushing Binodini and then back at Dash who was tottering on his heels, "She wished aloud for you to win, and it came true," said Dash.

The Raibahadur called for a toast and all gathered around. Raising his glass, he said, "I wish to thank a very charming lady for today's win and my dear friend here for all his support." All clapped and congratulated. Beral Babu for the first time in his thirty years of life felt a sense pride as he had gotten so used to people taking him lightly and even looking down upon him that he had forgotten the very essence of pride and honour. Today, in front so many people, he had come alive once more….. Birth of a new man…. His friend had restored and awakened that lost pride of his.

A party was the popular demand, and the Raibahadurs were not the type to back off. Everyone was invited, the crowd was large and there were many distinguished guests, polo players and of course the Maharaja and Maharani of Raipur. Binodini was introduced to many a women since she was so close to the Raibahadurs; acceptance was not a problem. The party was held in the lawns, a champagne tower had been set up and Raibahadur climbed up a ladder and poured from a large bottle into the topmost glass. The heady nectar flowed freely and amidst clapping and whistling, it continued till all the glasses were full of champagne. Binodini did not at all like the taste if it, whereas Beral Babu just about managed to drink his, the cooks of the palace had just excelled themselves this time. Lamb, chicken and fish were the order of the day; Binodini was amazed at the different ways in which the cooking was being done—the lamb was being slowly cooked on a large pit of glowing coal, the fish was grilled on spit fire and served with sauce, and there was a large iron tawa on which the chicken were being sautéed in ghee. For Beral Babu who loved his food, this was a wonderful culinary experience; he enjoyed tasting everything and Binodini joined him quite happily. Fluffy pineapple waffle was served with warm chocolate as the sweet dish at the end of the course and oh yes, there was also ice cream with freshly made hot, steaming pantuas.

At last, after most of the guests had left, the Raibahadur with a slim cheroot in hand was blowing out spirals into the air, a happy satisfied man after the days hard win, a tall elegant bespectacled gentleman came up. "Doc, where have you been? Come my good man… join me for a smoke," said the Raibahadur.... Small talk followed in which Beral Babu also joined in. "Where are you going for the pujos this time? I came to know that the children have gone to Europe, are you planning on joining them?" asked the doctor.

"I am thinking of going to my ancestral home...I made a promise that I would celebrate pujo there if I won this match, and it has been quite some time that I visited my village. The village pradhan wanted to discuss a few problems with me too."

Lady Sreelata, sitting next to him, did not look very pleased. "I have promised the children to join them and we have not been there in ages; it will need a lot of work and effort to celebrate pujo there.....I am not sure I would like to come."

Not looking very happy either, the Raibahadur said, "You do not have to come; go join the children and I will follow later. I would love to invite my good friend and his wife to join me in this endeavour of mine and doc.... you too are invited. It is decided than that we will leave on the fifteenth of this month.... that will give us a few extra days in hand to set up things there." The doctor laughingly declined saying pujo was the time when he had too many patients to take care off.

Beral Babu was at loss for words, caught off guard at that moment; he did not have the heart to decline such an invitation coming from his most gracious host who had shown such kindness and affection.

The return journey was quite uneventful.... Binodini enjoyed the ride and was very happy with the thought that she will be after all going somewhere for the pujo, whereas, Beral Babu, a creature of fixed habits and routine, was wondering how he would manage this disruptive journey.

Every one of us is governed by the Kalchakra that has its fantastic ways of governing and shaping our destiny.

7. Doubts and Concerns

Beral Babu looked at the 'Grande dame' today; it seemed as if the hour hand was just refusing to move….time was lying heavy on his hands when suddenly a very nasal voice from the next table disturbed his thoughts; it was none other than Bakshi mahasay, a very irritating inquisitive fellow. Bakshi was short, squat and totally egg bald…. no I am a bit wrong there; he did have a few strands on the top, every now and then he would fish out a comb from his pocket and give polish to these few imaginary strands.

Bakshi firmly believed in the saying that 'all work and no play makes Jack a dull boy', and so deep-rooted was his belief that in the last ten odd years of his service, he had never received a single promotion. That did not bother him much as long as he had a pay packet to carry home. Some in the office said he had married into money but Beral Babu had his own personal doubts as the poor state of his clothes and his habit of borrowing small changes, which he never returned, clearly contradicted the fact of his having any money at all.

Bakshi as usual had no work to do; hence, Beral Babu a sweet soul was a classical victim for entertainment. Leaving his own desk, he came across and leaned over Beral Babu's rickety old desk that was already groaning under the heavy weight of unfinished files.

"Ki Beral Babu, not getting any work done today….you seem to be in deep contemplation about something…maybe a low life like me can be of some help."

Beral Babu did not at all like being made fun of; he glared at Bakshi hoping he would move away, "Why don't you go to your own desk and allow others to finish their work? Everyone does not enjoy your kind of luxury," said Beral Babu sarcastically.

Bakshi was a little taken aback at this aggressive unfriendliness but people like him who have a cowhide for a skin never bother about sticks and stones thrown at them. Rubbing his hands gleefully as if he was going to unravel the world's seventh wonder, he continued absolutely confident that he would get the better of Beral Babu and some wholesome entertainment for himself.

Beral Babu just had enough and the most unexpected thing happened that day; he stood up and shouted at Bakshi asking him to go his way.

Thereafter, the garrulous Babus fell silent; after this episode, most spoke only in whispers and avoided coming anywhere near Beral Babu.

That day, Beral Babu took the five fifteen tram; he was travelling alone as Badai da had already taken leave, and had gone home to Jalpaiguri.

The tram was slow yet had its own benefits. It was not crowded and he got a window seat; he watched fellow humans struggling for existence. Struggle had become a part of one's life.

Might be there is no harm in going at all...after all they were going with the Raibahadur himself, It will do them both some good.

Somewhere in the bitter battle to just exist, he had lost the will to enjoy life, getting caught in the vicious cycle of pleasing others at the cost of his own personal relationship. Being just alive was not enough...alive and happy was the order of the day.

As he trudged home, the only thought that mattered to him most was to see his Binoo happy and smiling, somewhere in the hustle bustle of life he had just forgotten how much she mattered to him.

Swinging the ripe Hilsa in one hand, and his office satchel in the other, he entered home with one happy thought.....tomorrow was a Sunday.

Sunday was hectic for Binodini and saw a flurry of activities in the Beral household...Binodini did a thorough cleaning of the house....

after all they were going away for almost ten odd days. She washed, cleaned, and washed some more.

After lunch, while Beral Babu got hold of Majumdar to get some painting work done, she got busy in the kitchen. She tried out some of her grandmother's age-old recipes. After all, she could not go empty-handed and it was a pleasure cooking for Raibahadur as he was extremely appreciative of the various mishtis that she had been making for him.

She mixed roasted til to a warm mixture of brown sugar, spices, and dry fruits and rolled them out into soft round balls on a greased brass tray. The milk had already thickened to a dry consistency when she added khoya and powered cashew. This was then rolled out on a greased plate and cut into small squares.

She also made spicy namkeen snacks, some of which were also Beral Babu's favourite and she packed them into small neat packets so that they could be easily carried on the journey.

The next day, at the office when Beral Babu went to the section officer with a leave application, the old chap gave a sharp long look at Beral Babu and said, "Are you really?....good, I am glad you are."

A more confident Beral Babu was appreciated by many in the office, whereas in some quarters it was felt that he had become a bit too bold for his own good. During lunch, he no longer sat alone; he preferred the company of some of his good friends who appreciated this change in him.

He no longer travelled in the red beast, the tram though slow yet was more comfortable and soon he made quite a few friends among his fellow travellers. He realised one thing—smile and the world smiles with you.

When Beral Babu reached home that evening he saw Binodini very, very upset.

"Tell me.... and see how I solve it in seconds," said Beral Babu with a twinkle in his eyes.

"See the state of our suitcase.... it is coming off at the hinges and the jhola is also torn..... the only decent looking trunk we had, Rangamashi has taken it and has left her torn bag here."

Binodini was indeed right.... the only solitary suitcase they had, had seen better days since their marriage, and the jhola, though had been washed repeatedly, did give away a peculiar animal stink.

This was indeed a very serious problem; Beral Babu had a quick cup of tea and then slipping on his shoes, he went over to the vets.

After a little while, he returned with a nice big leather suitcase that was roomy enough to hold all their stuff and more. On Binodini enquiring as to from where he had got it, Beral Babu winked mischievously and said, "An old debt paid in full."

Her friends dropped in the next day and coming to know about her trip felt happy for her; they were leaving the very next day and there was still a lot of work to be done. Beral Babu paid a visit to the drycleaners on his way home and Binodini dealt with the very reluctant dhobi.

"Any news from the Raibahadurs?" asked Binodini.

"No, nothing," replied Beral Babu as he continued to read the old Bengali daily.

"What about our going, he had told the fifteenth of this month, had he not?" she said again drawing his attention.

"Has he forgotten...?" she said wistfully, her sad voice made him look up again; he also had started to feel the same little niggling doubts but he did not want to upset her.....let the fairy tale last as long as it can.

Instead, he said, "Let's wait and see; as far as I know him, he is not to be taken lightly."

Beral Babu continued to read the newspaper while Binodini finished her last bit of packing.

The next morning, Beral Babu walked over to his neighbour, a fine gentleman who worked in the government hospital requesting him to keep an eye on their house.

On being asked where he was going, Beral Babu sounded extremely vague about his destination for he too had started sharing Binodini's doubts.

Afternoon passed quickly.... still no message.

Tara, who was leaving for Darjeeling in the evening mail, came over to ask if she wanted anything particular from the hills. She watched Tara leave and felt envious.... at least her friend was going whereas she was no longer so sure.

Binodini hurried out to collect the towels that she had hung outside to dry.... the sky had darkened.... seemed like it would rain.

Towards evening, a slight drizzle had started that gradually turned into a heavy downpour; it was almost six in the evening. Beral Babu watched Binodini looking at the clock frequently, peeping out of the window at the slightest sound of any passerby.

Loud thundering followed the brightly lit up sky, even the lights went off. Lighting a small oil lamp, she went to sit near the window; her heart sank with a heavy sense of brooding. Won't they be going..... no news yet....she looked at the darkened skies that exactly matched her dark mood.

After a while, Beral Babu came out of the bedroom; he found her sitting quietly by the window, her mood matching the gloomy weather outside.

He felt sad and so very helpless.....

He so badly wanted to do something that would bring the smile back on her face.

8. A Journey in the Night

The hour ticked by very quickly, the 'Grande dame' showed half past eight and with each passing moment her gloom deepened....today she hadn't even remembered to give a cup of tea to her husband...their packed bags a glaring reminder of their not so impending journey.

Beral Babu felt extremely worried.... if things do not work out as planned... he started thinking of a suitable alternative...

To change her mood and distract her, he went near her and drawing her close to him he said, "See I am already ready.... you should too, it is already time for us to leave for the station; it is quite some distance from here and it will take us about a quarter of an hour to reach on time."

She let out a deep sigh of despair and clung to him tightly, and hiding her face in his broad chest she mumbled, "What's the point in making such an effort.... he has forgotten I am sure...."

Just then, the sound of hooves and the grinding crunch of the wheels of a buggy stopping in front of the gates was heard, this was followed by a deep steady knock on the main door.

Beral Babu picked up the oil lamp and hurried to open the door. "Sorry sir I am late...bad weather," said the smiling Dilbur Singh, a tall burly, deep throated chap. Tonight he was not much his regal self, soaked to the skin, his proud moustache hanging limply on his face.

"Your tickets," handing Beral Babu a small, sleek white envelope. "We have to hurry; the roads are flooded and we might have to take a detour." Picking up their suitcase, he hurried outside.

With a cry of delight, Binodini asked her husband to give her the lamp as she hurriedly got dressed in the dark bedroom. She covered herself with a light woollen shawl as she hurried outside.... due to the heavy rain it was slightly nifty outside. Her husband quickly shuttered all the windows, locked the main door, and padlocked the gate. Helping Binodini to climb the high steps of the buggy and settling her comfortably, they were off.

As the carriage moved towards its destination, the heavy downpour played a fierce tandem on the wooden roof. The roads were deserted other than a few brave souls; through the glass windows Binodini looked at the dreary and damp world outside. A happy smile played on her lips, the dark gloomy night gave a mysterious and intriguing touch to their journey.

"Oh! My God I forgot to give you a cup of tea today...." A very guilt ridden Binodini looked at her husband...who but just laughed aloud, "Do not worry so.... I will survive.... have heard that they not only serve tea and coffee but have a nice diner in these classes."

"Oh no! What about the food I am carrying?" Beral Babu laughed and planting a kiss on her soft cheeks, said, "I will eat that too."

The platform too had a deserted look, the usual hustle and bustle was missing only a few scattered souls here and there, Dilbur Singh handed them an umbrella and they hurriedly took shelter in the waiting room. Their first class waiting room had only one other traveller.

Dilbur Singh came in with their luggage. "Sir, please sit here; I shall look for the munshi who was supposed to be here to receive you both."

"What a terrible weather, I am really feeling like having a cup of tea...." her husband smiled indulgently and wiping his wet hair with a with a handkerchief, he went out into the platform.... it was totally deserted and dimly lit by the flickering lamps, only the brave old station master could be seen at a distance standing by his office.

"It seems there is not a single chaiwala anywhere.... can't see a single soul in this stormy weather," said Beral Babu on returning to the waiting room empty handed.

After a while, Dilbur Singh came in followed by a short turbaned man, his swarthy skin showed dark against the stark whiteness of his uniform, which had large damp patches. He seemed a little worried as he informed "Lady Sreelata had a small accident while riding....Raibahadur will be joining you a day later.... he has requested you to continue.... all arrangements have been made; the caretaker and the munshi of the of Hindol kothi will be there to receive you at the station."

The train was almost an hour late.... they ensured their seating. The first class coupe was extremely comfortable, the British knew how to travel in style, and the coupe was a class apart. Binodini explored its own private bath and toilet, there were matching towels in white, small bars of scented soaps and soft paper napkins near the hand basin, two large brass taps marked hot and cold.... placed under the taps were enamel buckets and a very large mug of the same.

There was still some time for the train to leave the station, many weary travellers were getting down.... hardly anybody getting in, the butler a foggy old man provided them with clean bed sheets, blankets and pillows they made themselves comfortable, "Would you like some tea or coffee, sir?" asked the waiter.

Sipping the hot steaming liquid from large china cups marked with the monogram of Indian railways, they waited.

The train had just started to move when the large glass door slid open to admit just one other traveller, the same gentleman they had seen in the waiting room. The steam engine blew furious blasts of smoke and the loud horn broke through the thundering and rain. As the train picked up speed cutting through the thick fog and rain, Beral Babu settled himself with a newspaper while Binodini propped a pillow behind her and settled herself next to the window trying to see beyond the darkness, soon the flickering lights of the city was left behind and a hallowed darkness engulfed the speeding train.

"They serve nice hot dinner in these classes." Beral Babu who was trying to read the newspaper in the moving train looked up at his co-traveller and smiled, "Yes I too have heard.... but it is our first time and we are carrying something packed."

The stranger seemed to be very tall with endless long legs, a head of oily hair parted in the centre, broad framed spectacles perched on his sharp nose and he was neither fair nor dark. He was extremely well dressed in white slim fitting pants and dark grey coat. Taking out a small silver box from his black leather handbag, he took out a pan and very ceremoniously biting off the end popped it into his mouth. "Some pan," offering to them both.

"I made these beauties with my own sweet hands," he said on their refusal to take any.

"I am Patta Nath Mishra"... the stranger introduced himself. Beral Babu found him to a very fine gentleman, and gradually they become quite friendly with him.

He was a resident of Darimbari; he was serving the royal family of that place for a very, very long time now; being their munshi, he took care of their business that involved a lot of travelling. "What about you Beral Babu, where are you going?"

Beral Babu said, "We too are going to Darimbari."

"Where too?" asked Mishra looking very surprised.

"We are going to Hindol kothi... we are the Raibahadur's guests."

Mishra hit his broad forehead with the palm of his hand and biting his tongue with his pan stained teeth he shook his head unbelievingly.

"You are the special guests I have been sent to receive, escort, and guide safely to your destination."

Whatever apprehensions Beral Babu had felt about this journey just melted away like mist in the rising sun.

Mishra was an extremely garrulous person and he had many an interesting tale to tell about the Rajas and their love-hate relationship with the Goras.

The fierce battles fought by the Pikas against the invaders on the sacred ground of kalingas. The way he described the battles, one could well imagine the gory details.

"On one hunting expedition I was sitting behind our Raja on the elephant and it got gored by another rogue elephant…. the raja took out his gun and…."

Binodini listened wide-eyed; such tales were exciting to hear on such dark stormy nights and added a sprinkle of mystery.

The three chatted like long lost friends; after a little while the ticket checker turned up; he was an Anglo Indian sahib of vague origin who spoke in heavily accented English, he did check their tickets but completely ignored Patta Nath…. did not even glance at him….

On seeing Beral Babu's questioning look, Mishra said, "I travel on the same train very frequently; I am a known face and being the Raja's munshi has its added benefits."

Dinner was a varied fare; it consisted of not only the mundane railway food but also included Binodini's hand cooked dry lamb meat flavoured with varied spices, curd, and cooked over low charcoal fire in a sealed wide-mouthed earthen pot. Small circular luchis rolled out of flour and deep-fried in ghee were the only complimentary accompaniment.

As the couple retired for the night in their comfortable bunks, they watched Mishra securing the glass door properly and drawing the heavy curtains. "We will be soon passing through the borders…. robbers….cutthroats…and bandits…one should be cautious…."

Sleep was a little difficult to come; Binodini kept looking outside through the window all she saw was vast stretches of darkness sometimes broken by even darker shapes of trees and mountains. The train had picked up speed to make up for the earlier delay and with all that sound and rolling movement, Binodini kept awake for quite some time.

She fell asleep and the last sound that she remembered was the rhythmic snoring of her husband crisscrossed by that of Mishra.

The next morning was bright and sunny; Mishra was already up and ready reading a hardbound novel….

"Good morning, welcome to the beautiful stretches of Orissa.... seeing you both sleeping so peacefully I did not have the heart to wake you up.... I took the liberty to order breakfast."

Breakfast consisted of bread and omellete accompanied with a dab of butter and jam, the tea was piping hot served in a large kettle covered with a deep blue teacozy.

While the men chatted, Binodini settled with a cup of tea near the window, the countryside of Orissa was totally different from the green plains of Bengal. Here and there were tall mountains dotting the skyline, one saw long stretches of rich green rice fields with scattered villages, large meandering rivers and the wide coastal areas with their sunny golden beaches. Yes.... truly a land of scenic beauty.

"You like our countryside, madam?" Binodini just loved the dramatic way in which Mishra addressed her.

"Yes, the countryside is so similar yet different." Hugging her woolen shawl closer and giving a little shiver, she said, "It is colder too."

Mishra just smiled seeing her give a little shiver; Binodini was dressed in a cotton sari that was not much of a protection against the cold. She was wearing a grey colour sweater with collars raised against her soft cheeks as if seeking protection against the chill, a light shawl that she had wrapped around herself tightly was teemed with a pair of large cotton socks borrowed from her husband.

"Where we are heading to is a mountainous area; hence, gets a trifle little colder during the winters, but this is the time to visit Orissa, see Jagannath Puri and the wide blue expanse of Chilka lake or even visit the Konark temple on the shores of the vast blue ocean."

The journey was extremely enjoyable and Mishra kept them enthralled with stories of shikar and adventure.

It was late in the evening that the train slowed down a wee bit due to the uphill track; it was cold and foggy. "We will be reaching late in the night, please do not worry. All necessary arrangements have been made."

Beral Babu looked at Mishra and said, "With you to guide us, I am not worried even a wee bit....if Raibahadur is late in coming, we will need your help to make the arrangements for the pujo....that is how he wants it."

"We will be arriving soon; the train will stop only for a few minutes ...I will take the luggage sir, you help madam down."

The fog had thickened making it difficult to decipher anything outside...Binodini pressed her nose against the cold glass trying hard to catch the glimpse of a light against the dark evenness of the night.

The train came to a sudden unexpected grinding crunch. "Our stop".

Mishra hurried outside with the large suitcase while Beral Babu helped his wife alight safely... they had not even made it to the last steps when the train started to move again.

"They should give some time to the passengers to alight....rogues," said Beral Babu in a huff.

"I know sir but since hardly anyone ever gets down here so....." said Mishra.

Binodini looked around and saw indeed the station was extremely small, just a tin shed....in the darkness of the foggy night, she could make out a few wooden benches. The stationmaster's room was in complete darkness. Not even a flicker of light anywhere....the cold was bone chilling, she slipped her hand into her husband's a sense of apprehension gripped her....sensing it Beral Babu drew his wife closer as if reassuring her that all was fine. She looked at the train whistling at a distance the last little flicker of light gone...an overwhelming sense of aloneness and desolateness descended on them.

Beral Babu must have also felt a little unsettled. "Where is the station master?" he asked.

"Oh! That old frog must have fallen asleep...it is hardly a station, the Raja himself had built it during the riots....easy for our soldiers to board trains during times of war," said Mishra.

A slight breeze had picked up its wings, the fog had thickened considerably and swirled around them menacingly....the cold silence of the night was getting unbearable.

Mishra stood close to them as if trying to shield them from unseen dangers, extremely alert to even the slightest sounds.

"Ancient route for thugs.... robbers and cut throats, they are rampant in these parts," he said almost in a whisper, the heavy fog seemed to drown his voice.

"What!"...Beral Babu exclaimed worriedly.

"Do not worry, I am armed to take care of any such emergency." Patting his side reassuringly, he said, "Your safety is of prime importance... the Raja himself has instructed."

Suddenly, as if from nowhere breaking the deep darkness of the night a loud voice was heard, raising high...the large lantern that he was carrying...throwing warm friendly light in the otherwise gloomy darkness of the small station, "You are late; I have been waiting since the last few hours."

The fellow was very tall and his large heavy frame was wrapped in a heavy woolen blanket that he carried with the ease of a shawl, his face could hardly be seen under all that hair, he had a mouthful of moustache and beard. Seeing the looks on their faces, Mishra tried to humour them by saying, "Looks like a dacoit," his words sending fearful shivers down Binodini's spine she held on more tightly to her husband's arm this action of hers was not missed by studied eyes.

The fellow laughed loudly than said very firmly yet politely, "I was named Sher Khan by the Raja himself....will see you safely to the palace....these are my orders." Picking up their luggage as if made from feather, he held the lantern aloft showing the way out.

Throwing a fleeting glance behind them at the engulfing darkness, they followed the tall figure out, Mishra coming in the rear and keeping a sharp look out. The fog was so thick it was difficult to even see a few steps ahead of them. It was amazing that

Khan knew which way to go, there was exactly no platform as such and the ground was uneven and rocky, full of bushes and thick thorny grass. Binodini was having a tough time walking....her sari got caught in the innumerable thorny bushes.....Beral Babu supporting her as they tried to keep up with Khan. Just then there was a loud blood curdling cry....Khan stopped and lowered his lantern to the ground, Patta Nath came ahead looking extremely alert, he held his finger to his lips, all froze to the imminent danger, he had fished out his pistol and was ready to fire. Khan kept their luggage down and indicating them to stay put, he drew out a large curved sword from under his blanket and disappeared into the swirling fog.

The defining silence was suddenly broken by the sound of heavy footfalls.... a voice was heard, "Tread not on paths so bravely where Bagha hunts."

"Sardar, there is a man and a woman..."

Mishra was shielding them with his body; Binodini's eyes were tightly closed, and she clung to her husband, Beral Babu knew they were in grave danger. He could feel Binodini shivering, instinctively he picked up a large rock lying near his feet.

There was sound of scuffle and steel against steel...

Fall of a heavy body on the ground and the terrible sound of sword being drawn against flesh....as if someone trying to breathe but chocking and straining......then ear deafening silence.

"They have killed Khan..." whispered Binodini chocking on her tears.

The fog made it impossible to see anything beyond a few footfalls and it seemed Mishra did not want to leave their side as that would leave them vulnerable....they waited unable to render any help...they would be attacked...for sure....

"That will teach you thugs a lesson not to meddle with the Raja's guests....next time I will make sure none of you...."

Beral Babu dropped the stone he was holding and Patta Nath put back the pistol in his shoulder holster with a wide smile on his face said, "Khan does it every time."

From the swirling mass of fog, Khan appeared; not a hair out of place and as if nothing had happened, picked up their luggage and the lantern nonchalantly guiding them out.

There was horse-drawn carriage waiting for them the driver was trying to calm down a large black horse that was pawing the earth with his hooves and neighing loudly.

As Binodini was helped up the short steps, she felt being watched. Inside she sat close to her husband drawing her shawl tightly around her, the carriage had a cloth hood yet was quite warm and comfortable and Mishra sat opposite to them, whereas, Khan sat with driver in the front, the large lantern swung from its post where it was hung as the great beast put speed into his hooves.

The road was just but a mud track with thick jungle on both sides. Even beyond the fog, one could make out tall trees as if trying to touch them with long outstretched arms. The windowpanes of the carriage had turned misty and one could hardly see anything outside except distant dark shapes.

The driver could be heard encouraging the great animal.... Who was sure footed and possessed great strength. A light drizzle had started and the carriage swung a few times dangerously on the uneven track.

"Hope the earlier incident did not scare you too much...."spoke Mishra. "We are used to dealing with these thugs....extremely dangerous....not human at all," he continued. "It was extremely brave of you today sir....I saw you with stone...you are a fighter, sir."

Beral Babu mumbled something indistinguishable he himself had never thought he would react as he did. In the dark interior of the carriage, though one could not see each other's face, Binodini did look at her husband with great respect, this side of his she never knew.

Nothing-missed Mishra's eyes….he knew that the Maharaja would be pleased.

The road seemed to have become uphill as they moved a bit slower now, the great horse straining against odds. "We should get down; the poor animal is finding it difficult," said Binodini.

"Very gracious madam but Nestor is an amazing horse; do not worry," said Mishra. The carriage passed through the large gates of the palace and the wheels seemed to have hit a gravelled pathway… "We are approaching the Palace; welcome to Hindol kothi and the land of the Kalinga Rajas," said Mishra.

The carriage had stopped under a large portico supported by several tall columns; the great horse was blowing funnels of fumes after his exertion; the palace itself was of massive proportions but the darkness was so overwhelming that it was difficult to see much. After her terrifying experience at the station, Binodini stayed close to her husband; there was not a single flicker of light anywhere. "Where is Gobordhan….did you not inform Khan…he will answer to me today," as if in cue hearing Mishra's angry voice, "Hujoor, please forgive my delay…in fact I was waiting near the gates and saw you pass."

Gobordhan was well-wrapped against the cold and all that running made him breathe hard. As he held aloft the lantern he was carrying, in the flickering light of the lantern Binodini could make out the large number of red stone stairs that led to the main door, there were two large statues of Gargoyles at the head of the stairs as if ready to pounce on unsuspecting visitors. Khan got busy taking out their luggage whereas Gobordhan held aloft the lantern to guide them up the stairs.

Binodini left her husband's side and went close to the big black majestic animal and placing the palm of her hand on his neck, she patted him and said, "Thank you, Nestor." On hearing his name being called, he turned his majestic head and looked down at her with his large liquid brown eyes; then suddenly throwing back his great head he neighed loud and clear into the deepness of the night.

Beral Babu drew Binodini away from the horse "Come, they are waiting for us." They climbed the stairs and approached the great door of brass and teak. Mishra pulled on the rope knocker and waited, there was no response, he turned towards Gobordhan and said angrily, "It seems you all are sleeping...you all will deal with me tomorrow."

A fearful Gobordhan could just about say, "I had informed Shibram to wait here...seems he must have slept off."

"You all have become like ghosts... appear and disappear at will... .I will sort you...."

Enough was said, the massive door opened and a diminutive dhuti clad well turbaned man stood with his hands folded respectfully in front of the guests but he fearfully moved away from Mishra's angry countenance.

They were led into a small saloon, there was a warm log fire in the fireplace and hot tea was served to them by Gobordhan.

9. Hindol Kothi

The steaming brew brought life back into their cold shivering limbs, and Binodini gratefully sank into one of the high backed leather bound chairs near the dancing flames.

"Sir, I will inform the Maharaja of your safe arrival and khan will see to your luggage," said Mishra. Beral Babu was quite exhausted and hungry…

The large variety of biscuits and small cocktail sandwiches served with tea was extremely filling. Warm and contended they waited but only for a little while….Mishra came back to guide them to the Maharaja's presence.

As they entered the great hall, both of them were amazed by its grandeur and opulence. It was in stark contrast to the drabness of the outside of the palace. High ceilings painted in gold and supported by tall columns that ended as lotuses at their bases. The walls had motifs of peacocks, horses and dancing girls, hanging from the ceiling was a single crystal chandelier that was lit with a thousand wicks enough to light up such a hall of massive proportions.

In the light of the chandelier, the walls of the room glittered because of the precious gems that adorned the various paintings and motifs. The furniture meant to seat a hundred odd guests were Baroque French styled gold painted chairs with delicate glass topped centre tables

The floor was made out of white marble, here and there near the sofas and the chairs were thick Persian rugs of multitude colours. As they were guided by Mishra they passed a section of the wall decorated with hunting trophies…there were large massive heads of bison, wild boar, nilgai, and deer of many species….these were complimented by weapons of many types on the walls.

"It seems you like my hunting trophies…..shot these beauties on my various hunting trips," the strong male voice belonged to a man who was standing on a tiger skin rug….he was tall and old yet very regal, his broad frame was covered by the finest silk….dhuti and a loose jacket with red gold tassels, he wore large kundals of gold in his earlobes, his hair had many touches of grey and lay in a sleek style beyond his shoulders. With his aristocratic bearing he could have been none other than his highness Maharaja Gajapati Singh Deo.

Both Beral Babu and his wife touched his feet with great respect… raising him and holding him by the shoulders, the Maharaja looked at Binodini and said, "Your husband is a very brave man….no one till now has ever thought of fighting these thugs with just a stone…a man of very rare courage indeed."

The Maharaja smiled his dark eyes shone kindly on the couple standing before him, and then, turning to Mishra he said, "You both have done well….I am pleased… as for the thugs…. send the soldiers tomorrow."

"It is late…. way beyond midnight; Mishra will show you to your rooms. Tomorrow is special…. the Maharani has been waiting to meet you both."

They were led away from the Maharaja's presence by Gobordhan and Mishra. They entered a long corridor deeply carpeted and well lit with small crystal oil lamps fixed on both sides of the walls, there were no empty spaces on the walls, paintings of regal ancestors andfavourite horses filled the walls.

The corridor opened into a dining hall, it was of comfortable proportions, the dining table was long and polished black with a sitting capacity of twenty odd persons, silver candle holders gleamed in the light of the overhead chandeliers. The floor was black granite and the walls were wooden paneled and bare.

"That is the kitchen there," said Gobordhan pointing to a large door in polished teak….

"All the living quarters are upstairs," Mishra pointed to a wide marble staircase that had railings of brass that shone like gold.

"I hope you are not hungry; otherwise Gobordhan here can make some soup." They had their fill of biscuits and sandwiches, and hence, refused.

At the head of the staircase there were two large cupids pointing in opposite directions, "We shall take the right cupid better to remember otherwise it is very easy to lose one's way in a palace of these proportions".

Stopping in front of a large wooden door, which had two large brass knobs in the shape of two white doves, as he turned the knobs to open the door, Mishra said, "Every door has knobs shaped in the form of different animals, you must remember yours otherwise like last time...we had a lady guest...General John Mason's wife who by mistake entered the room of our crown prince....extremely embarrassing affair it was...."

"If you need anything just pull this cord," pointing to a red gold rope hanging near the door. "Gobordhan here will attend to whatever you need." The door opened as he turned the knobs the beauty and grandeur of the room left Binodini speechless. "The Maharani herself assigned your room....fit for a queen, madam."

"Your luggage has been already unpacked sir, have a good night."

Patta....make sure my guests are safe...they are special...you know that already I am sure....this is the last test....he has promised us all a place at his feet....freedom at last...I am weary....a clean slate of life....." Mishra heard with his head bowed with respect. "I will ensure it; please do not worry," he said as he left the great presence to do his contemplation.

"This room is so beautiful, my grandmother used to tell stories about fairies and princess who lived in castles....." the walls were a powder blue with painted patterns of creepers and vines in gold, the ceiling was high with a round dome that pointed down wards in the shape of a lotus and from its centre hung a beautiful crystal chandelier that lit up the room with a thousand wicks, the windows were large and covering them were heavy drapes in brocade and silk in deep sea blue, in front of the fire place was an arrangement of silk cushions on a large blue gold Persian carpet, the floor was made out of marble with inlays of gemstones of many hues....at the centre of the room was a large four poster with snowy lace drapes.

Beral Babu seeing her so happy smiled, "It is very late...where are our clothes?...."

Opening the doors of a large cupboard, Binodini found all their clothes pressed and laid out neatly, in a chest of drawers she found his socks and other smaller items.

"Where is the bathroom I wonder..." said Binodini.

"Going to explore everything in one night?" teased Beral Babu.

Binodini picked up a clean sari and went to wash and change, the bathroom was small. The walls were an extension of the bedroom, there was a large bath tub carved out of jade, and next to it, were glass tables of very low height on it were placed scented soaps in soap dishes made out of crystal that glinted and let out colours of the rainbow as they caught the light coming from the large lamps of brass with glass domes fixed on the adjacent walls.

The towel rack near the long gilded mirror on the wall held soft fragrant towels of pink and blue. The porcelain basin had a marble counter that held scented oils in small vials of rose and white quartz. On one side was a balloon shaped bottle that contained sandal wood powder; it had a large round wooden stopper and was carved out of laborite that gleamed with a multitude of colours. Placed next to it was a small mixing bowl of the same with a silver spoon.

She pulled on the blue gold cord hanging from the wall that turned out all the lights of the chandelier just as Mishra had said it would do.

The only warm glow in the room was from the fireplace. As she turned the silk coverlet of gold and blue Binodini smiled a happy smile to herself….she sank into the softness of the bed and pulled the eider down quilt to cover herself and Beral Babu who was already snoring rhythmically on his side of the bed.

The snowy lace drapes gave the feeling of floating in the clouds, the last thought on her mind as sleep overcame her…she thanked……

"Be alert…no slackness will be tolerated…..he failed once at the station but will try again…." A dark cloud rose from the palace grounds and slowly spread across filtering into each unseen crevices.

Two men bundled in warm shawls were hurrying up the hilly track…

"Look those lights again….do not venture there ever at this time of the night…"

"Let's go….seeing is also getting cursed," the two figures hurried towards the safety of their village.

The night was dark and the cold clammy fingers of the fog ran shiver down one's spine, "I can hear your teeth chattering."

"I am fine…..let us hurry."

The road was but just a track meandering through the mountain side on barefoot the going was difficult. The two men helped each other guessing each footfall.

"When you had left in the first place what made you come back…. you fool you will get me cursed too… if you had not been my sister's husband, I would ring your scrawny neck".

"I had no choice….received a telegram about the guests…."

"We stood in the station for almost half a day, checked every train and every passenger who got down…what else can you do?"

"I have to inform….think of the effort that I put in to get the rooms cleaned in the circuit house and all my effort has been wasted".

"So now you have suddenly become intelligent, where is that other fellow who works with you, he must have taken off as usual….

almost got me killed by trying to go there in the first place at this time..."

"Listen you have been angry enough....thought I should check.... never know these city people, they feel adventurous on coming to small places like this.... I shall be answerable if anything happens".

"Tomorrow first daylight you better inform the thanedar...."

"No not now, I will wait for news first."

The two figures stopped and took a breather on the outskirts of their village, the tiny flicker of lights coming from the chinks and crevices in the small thatched huts gave a feeling of safety and security.

"I hope they know the reason....why I could not come," said a very tired and sleepy Raibahadur. The day at the hospital was full of worry and tension, the injury being of serious nature.

"Of course, I have informed sir and I have also ensured their comfortable journey," said the munshi.

"Dilbur Singh, I want you to book our tickets on the first ship out of here for Germany; you both will be coming with me...munshi, contact my good friend Dr. Sneider, send a post to him quickly informing him about the situation....."

As the Raibahadur moved towards the wide spiraling marble stairs case....munshi hurried after him and asked, "But sir, what about our guests?"

"What about them?" asked the Raibahadur.

"Inform them that you won't be coming at all...?"

Wearily, the Raibahadur rubbed his fingers across his eyes, "Have you informed the munshi of the Hindol Kothi suitably?" Seeing the Munshi giving a vigorous nod to his question, "Then why worry? Let them enjoy their pujo holidays...but yes, do inform that fellow to take great care of both of them for I will not tolerate any kind of slackness on his part."

Time was something that they lacked; instructing Dilbur Singh about the tickets, the munshi hurried home.... the upper most thought on his mind was to send a telegram to Darimbari.

A loud knock on the small door... "Munshi wake up... her condition has worsened.....the Raibahadur has summoned you."

The munshi got hurriedly dressed regretting the whole affair of having continued working here....he should have taken up the government job his uncle had arranged for him....it was more paying too.

The doctor cast a serious look at the aristocratic gentleman standing in front of him.... "She has fractured ribs, which will take time to heal but that is not what I am worried about... it is her spinal injury which is beyond me, she will need an expert....if you can take her to Europe, she stands a fair chance."

"I am planning to take her to Germany.... We are trying to leave as early as possible and I am also taking my family doctor just in case."

On their way back to the palace, the Raibahadur's thoughts harboured on his wife's injured and inert frame..."What scared the horse to buck and kick out at the rider, that too inside the riding ring?" he quizzed Dilbur Singh who was in charge of all his horses.

"Prince is being ridden by our lady since the last five odd years.... he has never ever been unpredictable....trained him myself sir....I am myself disappointed...the sahees who was standing near the ring said something very strange.....a dark figure suddenly appeared and..."

On a warning look from the munshi, he went silent....Raibahadur noticed this and said angrily, "Munshi, if you hide anything from me, I will shoot you and no one will ever find your miserable body."

"Sir, we have to leave now... the ship leaves in about an hour." It was still dark outside when the Raibahadur left the palace.

The munshi hurriedly packed a few of his belongings and rushed to the port....in his hurry, the directions given by the Raibahadur totally slipped from his mind.

10. A Cherished Meeting

The loud peals of a mandir bell from a distance echoed in her ears… she woke up with a start then seeing her familiar surroundings she smiled and stretched like a sleepy cat, his side of the bed was vacant where did he go to….she wondered. The small face of the clock on the wall showed a quarter to seven, she picked up a change of clothes and rushed to the bathroom, someone had filled already drawn up a bath for her as the tub was filled with warm scented water….how very kind and thoughtful. The soap smelt of roses and melted on her skin as she rubbed herself, the water was pleasantly warm, back in her village early morning baths meant….getting up at the crack of dawn before the men woke up and summoning all her friends….always go in a group her mother would say never go alone she would warn. The group of girls would head for the pond with a change of clothes… before one took a dip shifting the algae, weeds and green scum that floated on the surface was to be done very, very carefully and for doing that the very bravest among them would venture first. The unlucky ones who carried a bundle of clothes would wash them first, whereas the few lucky ones, who had no such chores to do, would take a skinny dip. She dug in her toes into the warm bottom of the tub….no muddy or gooey feel there, smiling contentedly she closed her eyes.

She tied her sari the way all Bengali ginnis do, and then combed out her long black hair in front of the dressing table. She wandered how she should tie her hair, leave it in a braid, or make a khopa. The dressing table was large and matched the walls of the bedroom; it had three mirrors set side by side so that one could see one's reflection from all the three angles, on delicate lace coverlet were laid out combs of ivory and gold, a small silver mirror with a short handle, bottles of perfumes and attar were kept for her to use in the left drawer, whereas the right one held powders and lip balms. A small silver box held pins, and khopa clips of gold and silver studded with different types of precious gems.

She left her room and reached the stairs with its cupids pointing in two opposite directions. As she descended the stairs, a turbaned servant in a dhuti and achkan who was cleaning the lantern glasses wished her and continued with his chore. Then, she noticed that all the heavy drapes had been drawn to let in the bright sunlight. The crystals hanging from the large chandeliers gleamed letting off the colours of the rainbow.

Fragrance from lighted incense sticks and flowers floated in the air guiding her to the palace temple. As she climbed the stairs leading to the inner sanctum of the mandir, she heard voices and chiming of bells. There was a large statue of Goddess kali ready to battle with a sword in one hand and a beheaded head of an Asura in the other. Binodini folded her hands in reverence, and then kneeled in front of the Goddess seeking her blessings.

Beral Babu, who was already seated in a corner with Mishra, saw her and he beckoned to her to join him. The Raj pundit was a tall, thin, and shaggy-haired old man. He was very dark.... so dark that the pupils of his eyes appeared a bright white and he was bare bodied except for the sacred thread; dressed only in a red loin cloth, he was chanting mantras and doing the morning arati. The Maharaja was seated on a tiger skin wearing a white cotton punjabi teamed with a saffron dhuti; today his long hair was tied at the nape of his neck with a black satin ribbon. Seated on his right was a lady dressed in a honey brown tassar sari, her back was towards Binodini.

There were offerings of laddoos and sandesh in large brass thalis... flowers....garlands of lotus, marigold and rose adorned the Goddess.

They all stood and with folded hands waited for the pundit who after having finished the Arati came over to them with the sacred flame. First, he came to the Maharaja and the Maharani who after touching the flame with their open palms touched their own heads and face, and then bowed their heads in reverence. Others followed suit.

Binodini stood in a corner waiting....for others to finish when a voice rang in her ears... it sounded like the soft gurgling of a mountain stream....gentle and bubbly. The bearer of the voice was beautiful beyond any human comparison. Kalidas' Shankuntala or the apsara's of the heaven would have shied away in front of such grace and beauty. She came and stood in front of Binodini.....skin reddish white, hair raven black flowing in waves till her knees, doe-like eyes framed by delicately arched eyebrows, lips like two rose petals, there was a touch of white fire on her ear lobes, a single long string of black pearls hung from her neck and almost reaching her shapely waist.... her tall willowy persona left Binodini awestruck.

She came close, very close her sweet scented breathe framing Binodini's face.

Turning to Beral Babu who stood close by, she said, "Such a lovely girl...you have a very pretty wife." Both Binodini and Beral Babu touched her feet seeking her blessings.... "May you both get your heart's desire," was all that she said as she hugged Binodini close to her and bestowed a soft kiss on her forehead.

"You all must be famished... come, lets have breakfast," Gobordhan hurried ahead of them to see to the arrangements.

"Come son... sit on my right," the Maharaja asked of Beral Babu.

Binodini sat on the great table next to the Maharani ....breakfast consisted of fruits of various kinds some of which she had not even seen or tasted before; servants offered them small silver glasses of warm milk with dry fruits. "I hope you like this fare or would you like to have something else served?" asked the Maharani as if reading Beral Babu's mind who loved his luchis, mishti, brinjal fries, and Hilsa.

"I would love to partake what Binodini has made and got for us," said the Maharani. Gobordhan directed the servant to show the silver salver to the Maharaja and Maharani.

"A labor of love, a most apt gift for thirsty souls...." sighed the Maharani as she tasted a little of everything.

Mishra came close to the Maharaja and bowed respectfully, "The prince has arrived....with news."

The Maharani herself got up and laid out a place for the prince who walked in just then.

After greeting his parents in a very respectful and formal manner, he went close to his father and spoke in low undertones....it must have been of serious nature for she watched the Maharajas face turning grave and angry.

"Come now... no more of such talks for the moment....my son.... come... meet our guests," said Maharani.

Beral Babu got up from his place his face turning red with shyness and hesitation it was not every day that one dinned with royalty or got introduced to a prince. The prince Aditya Raj Singh Deo was very tall and towered over Beral Babu, broad shoulders, strong and lean built, his hair was curly and just about touched his shoulders, he wore black dhuti that fitted his long muscled legs leaving no loose ends...his body was covered with heavy armour and he held a plumed helmet in one hand...to Binodini he looked like those old, ancient folklore heroes from her school books who had just come from a hard fought battle.

As he turned and looked at her, he had a very charming smile on his handsome face...Binodini blushed a pretty pink, as he came close to her and greeted her.... she had never before had such attentions from a man so gallant.

Breakfast over, they all moved towards the small saloon next to the dining hall.

"Come Binodini, lets leave the men to themselves, I will show you around the palace."

As the two women left the saloon, Maharaja spoke for some time in muted tones with the prince while Mishra gave Beral Babu company showing some hunting trophies.... "Sir, this is the beast I was speaking to you about in the train….it almost would have killed us had not it been for the intervention of our elder prince."

Beral Babu who was eyeing the large stuffed tiger that still looked menacing even in death…. "Elder prince? Where is he?"

"Alas sir! Please forgive me… I am not free to speak about…but his absence causes great sorrow for both….I can say no more."

His words made Beral Babu wander as to what had happened to cause such great sorrow.

The two women left the saloon and through a long corridor they reached the mandir; servants who were discretely busy bowed in respect as the Maharani passed through. From here a large door opened to the outside, the sun was bright in the sky driving away the cold and fog of the previous night, the central courtyard of the palace was large and floored with large blocks of red sandstone, green soft mossy grass had creeped into the various crevices in between the slabs making their presence felt.

At the centre of the courtyard there was a large fountain…the water of the fountain fell in cascades from the mouth of a dragon and in the pool at the foot of the fountain were a large number of fairy fishes in the colours of green, gold, and blue, these swam about merrily in the little pool, there shiny scales reflecting the sun's light, their wing like fins spreading out like fans in the water as they swum around. Around the fountain sat a large number of fan-tailed white doves that flew away in a flutter of wings as they approached. The palace was constructed out of red sandstone. The upper stories housed the servants and the soldiers who guarded the palace. There were four tall towers at the four corners used as a lookout for enemies, Binodini could see soldiers with weapons guarding at various vantage points.

They passed through a large iron gate and entered the palace grounds that were lush green in colour. "Come this way… I want to show you something," said the Maharani.

A large black horse with white on three of his hooves stood grazing, a sahees in riding gear stood nearby....on seeing them approaching, he came in a run and bowed.

"You know him already... he is Nestor," said the Maharani. Binodini smiled; indeed she knew him.

The horse, on hearing his name, threw his great head back and neighed....then he trotted up to the Maharani who patted him and scratched his neck. "My baby.....missed you...I knew you would be tired....we will ride tomorrow, my friend, at the crack of dawn."

Talking to a horse so endearingly....Binodini did not find it strange. She herself often spoke in such endearing tones to the strays that she fed behind her kitchen garden.

"Nestor came to us as a foal...third generation of war horse presented to us by the Raja of Marwar. He is a Marwari horse...look how small his ears are and pointy too...known for their intelligence and endurance in the battlefield...he has ridden the Maharaja to quite a few battles...his cunningness in the battlefield has saved his life quite a number of times."

"Come let's move on," said the Maharani and they walked up the gravelled driveway. Maharani kept pointing out to various fruit trees and different varieties of flowering plants to her. Just then Gobordhan came huffing and puffing, "Maharaja sahib wants to know if your 'graceful nesses' would like to accompany them on partridge shooting."

"Let us hurry... we need to change." Binodini followed the Maharani back into the palace, but change? All she had were a few saris.

She stood in her room thinking of the various excuses that she could come up with.....Beral Babu walked in just then and saw her standing there looking worried.

"I hope you have packed my only pair of pants....can't go like this," pointing to his loose punjabi and dhuti.

"What shall I wear? I only have a few cotton saris." Just then a knock was heard on the door.

"Hujoor....Maharani Sahiba has sent these clothes for you," yet another maid standing behind the first laid out a selection of sturdy walking shoes on the floor.

"We have been instructed to help you to dress," said the first.

Beral Babu watched Binodini come down the stairs a little shyly in clothes she was unaccustomed to wear...a long tweed skirt teamed with a white shirt and a thick woolen sweater in grey, her feet safely ensconced in sturdy walking shoes...her long hair was braided into a neat plait and folded and retied again at the nape of her neck with a silk scarf. The prince standing close to him whispered in his ears, "Be careful... I might steal her...."

The men walked ahead while the women brought up the rear.... Mishra was his usual alert self.

"I told the Maharani not to take her to the maze today....she is not yet ready....tomorrow..." said the Maharaja to the prince.

"You are right...in doing so....but the curse....only a pure soul should seek the Akash Ganga....." asked the prince.

"So I hope....she is the one....tomorrow is the day," he said.

The walk through the forest was difficult, though not very far.... yet the trails did lead uphill making the going extremely difficult for Beral Babu....face beetroot red and sweating through every pore of his body, he tried to keep up with the prince's tall athletic frame.

They reached the river and the servants hurriedly pitched up umbrellas, and set up the chairs and tables. Sitting under the cool shade of an umbrella, Binodini watched the prince loading his gun..... seeing her stare, he came up to her and said, "Would you like to try?"

She abhorred the very idea of killing anything. "No... I do not feel like it."

Beral Babu noticed the prince speaking to her and he was not only shaking inside from his earlier exertion but now he felt totally weak in the knees from this unaccustomed shower of attention by the prince.

"My prince, if I may intrude I would like to try…though you have to show how?"

The servants formed a semicircle and started beating the bushes with sticks….from her seat under the umbrella Binodini could see scores of bird flying out. The men and the Maharani sahiba trying their luck. On that day beginners luck smiled on Beral Babu and before anyone else could he landed successful shots on wanted targets.

A very proud Beral Babu walked up to his wife, "Landed two of them…. see."

"Good show," praised the Maharaja and Maharani.

A lazy picnic under the sun was the most enjoyable experience that Binodini had ever had….back in her village during the hot summer afternoons she and a few of her friends would creep into the mango groove of the old koncha moshai then they would steal raw mangoes as many as they could…then sitting under the deep shades of the trees they would feast….of course the stomach cramps in the evening was a part of the whole deal….the stale bitter medicine that followed was punishment enough.

"Here Binodini, taste some roasted partridges….ones your husband has shot." The meat was soft and had a mild wood charcoal flavour to it, teamed with hot Indian bread baked over glowing embers on an iron tava tasted like god's offerings.

"Eat the bread with these green chilies fried in salted mustard oil," the Maharani herself served her a helping; the love and care that reflected on her face reminded Binodini of her mother.

After lunch, the men fought a hard battle over a game of chess. The prince was supported by the Maharani while Beral Babu learnt his moves from the Maharaja himself,……life is but a game of chess, learn your moves well and no one can beat you.

The sun was but just a glow of orange ball when they started towards the palace….going was easier. Beral Babu chatted happily with Mishra.

"In these jungles not many years ago tigers roamed freely but now....one can find only wild boars and bears which of course are no less dangerous."

"Patta....as usual scaring people with your tall tales," said the prince on seeing Beral Babu looking apprehensively into bushes and trees. It was already dark by the time they set foot inside the palace.

"Hujoor messenger has brought news....doctor sahib is coming with his wife and her sister."

The Maharaja smiled and said, "Aha! My good friend John Macintyre is coming....we will have a nice enjoyable evening today."

"I better retreat to the safety of my room before I am besieged," said the prince laughingly.

"Come, come young man thou shall not grudge the attentions of the fair kind."

They all laughed as they heard the Maharani teasing her son so.

All hurried to their rooms to get ready to receive their guests.

Not very far off from the palace two weary and tired men hurried as they walked on the meandering road on the hill side. It was a full moon night and going was easier.

"See, I told you there would be no one at the palace.....why I listen to your mad ideas I do not know.....if you were not married to my sister, I would have wrung your scrawny neck."

"Yes you are right....most probably they did not come only....but I had to check."

"Now if you tell me to come with you again....I swear by my sister I will ring that scrawny neck of yours."

"What you...I myself will not be coming back till the pujo is over....lets hurry it is getting late."

The two men hurried home.

Binodini sank into the warm bath, the day had been hectic and her whole body was aching from the day's walk through the jungle... Refreshed, she changed hurriedly into a cotton sari with a wide red border and teamed it with a blouse of the same colour. Combing out her hair into a neat plait, she slipped her feet into a soft crème coloured leather jootis, one among the many pairs that the maids had brought in that morning. A tired Beral Babu had to be literally coaxed by Binodini to get ready.

As they descended the stairs, the sound of laughter and voices floated up to them from the saloon, which was near the dining hall.

"I missed you so much....Europe was so cold and you were always in my mind," the voice was loud and screechy.

They entered the saloon just in time to receive the guests. The doctor was of medium height with a thatch of red brown hair, clean shaven and freckled face. The Maharaja hugged his friend and introduced him to his guests.

The owner of the screechy voice was none other than his wife Annabel Elizabeth Macintyre, taller than her husband by almost a foot; she was thin and had a very long face...she wore a white lace gown with a brown cape thrown over her shoulders. As she saw Binodini, she looked hard and gave a faint smile, her heavy lidded grey eyes and sharp beak-like nose gave the impression of a crane that looks hungrily at the fishes in the pond.

"This is Binodini.... I did write to you about their coming.....like a daughter to me....our special guests." On hearing this, Mrs. Macintyre's expression immediately softened into a warm friendliness.

In comparison to his wife, the doctor was extremely soft spoken and Beral Babu felt completely at ease in his friendly company. "My father was a general....I am the fourth son, came to India with the East India Company, served for many a years here, India grows on you...I fell in love with Darimbari and its beautiful Maharani and I could never ever leave," said the doctor as he twirled the warm brandy in the goblet.

"I understand what you mean; it is like mishti....one cannot just let go...the more you eat, the more you want." Beral Babu had never spoken so extensively before in front of a stranger.

"Ha! Here is a young man after my heart who loves his mishti as I do," said the doctor patting Beral Babu on the back.

After having stayed for so many years in India, both the doctor and his wife had an extensive knowledge of both Odisha and Bengali, and same was for the Maharaja and the Maharani who could fluently converse in as many languages.

White wine was served in tall crystal flutes with slender stems... Beral Babu who never ever drank anything stronger than tea picked up a glass on the Maharaja's insistence.

"Where is Lizzie....has she not come with you?" asked the Maharani...Lizzie was Mrs. Macintyre's sister; she was on her way on horseback....seemed had taken a little detour on her own to see the old mandir next to the river....

"That place is very beautiful...we can all go there...why not tomorrow?" said the Maharani....sitting close to her friend near the fire place.

"That would be lovely....John is so keen on fishing...right dahling!" she looked at her husband sitting right across next to Beral Babu on the sofa.

"You are so right, my deah! What about you Mr. Beral?"

A dreamy smile appeared on Beral Babu's face "I love my fish as much as the next man....hilsa, rohu, bhakur and tyangra are my favourites."

"Look my friend, here is a man after my heart," said the doctor to the Maharaja who was standing on a tiger skin rug near the divan on which Binodini was sitting and speaking to Mishra in closed hushed tones...Binodini could just about catch a few words...prince...cave. The Maharaja looked worried and tense.

Gobordhan entered the saloon and announced the arrival of Mrs. Macintyre's sister....the heavy fall of riding boots was heard and Lizzie walked into the saloon.

She was very unlike her sister….short and squat in built, she had extremely pale complexion and dark mousy brown hair…..round chubby face with pale blue eyes…..not bad at all.

She had a loud gurgling laughter as she spoke…. That sounded warm and friendly.

"Lizzie deah! You will be happy to know that the prince is back…. oh my, just see her blush!"

Lizzie hurried upstairs to change and freshen up while the others chatted.

"My friend, you look upset…any news about the prince?" asked the doctor….hearing him ask so….everyone in the room fell silent and looked at the Maharaja. Both the maharaja and the Maharani looked very upset.

Maharaja looked at both Binodini and Beral Babu, "I suppose there is no point in hiding from you both…sooner or later you will come to know. My eldest son was kidnapped when he was just but a child…all these years we have been trying to find him….our souls will not rest in peace till we free him…." The Maharaja could speak no more, and turned away and stood looking at the flames. The doctor and his wife rose from their seats and came near to him.

"We all are there with you in this, my friend," said the doctor.

"I am so sorry…being so late, I thought that I should change into something presentable," her bubbly entry and her gurgling voice cut through the sadness that hung in the room like a cloak.

She had indeed made an effort hair carefully coiffured into a French knot, her lips reddened a deep red and her wine colour gown added more colour to the Persian rug on which she sat down…..with a glass of wine in hand her eyes kept darting towards the door…. Binodini who was sitting close to her felt she was looking for someone or something.

Just then, the prince entered…bowing gallantly and wishing his guests….dressed in black pants and a white shirt, his long hair tied at the nape with a black ribbon….he looked amazing enough to steal one's breathe away…. he completely ignored Lizzie and looked at Binodini mischievously and said, "You are going to break my heart someday."

This shook up Beral Babu; his drink forgotten, all that he did the whole evening was keep a sharp eye on the prince …..and Lizzie seeing the whole thing, became more ardent in her pursuit, she did everything she could to get prince's attention.

"Lizzie, give us a song….it has been such a long time…let your song drive away all the sadness," said the Maharani.

She was more than happy enough to oblige, "God save the king, I will die young…" said the prince.

She first played on the piano for some time closing her eyes and nodding her head from side to side, than fixing her gaze on him, Lizzie opened her mouth wide and sang…..wooing the prince…she had a gruff voice that was not all in sync with the keys that she was playing….

"Here comes the royal torture…." The prince whispered…. almost in her ears…Binodini giggled….and Beral Babu sat up straight.

The two men sat down to the frugal fare of thick flat oven-hot bread and dal….the chullah burning merrily in the makeshift kitchen lent a bit of heat to the room….their wives having served dinner were sitting on the cot where their children lay asleep….the cold wind rattled the doors and windows. Just than the howling of wolves was heard.

The two men, though warmly wrapped in thick blankets, shivered.

"Coming from the jungles behind…"

"Yes…."

The two men sat close together keeping guard while the women and the kids slept.

A sumptuous dinner followed the musical evening, dishes were plentiful…roasted partridges stuffed with tiny button mushrooms, rohu cooked in a spicy gravy of onions and tomatoes...charcoal baked pomfrets wrapped in lotus leaf....exotic dishes of lamb and roasted venison. The dining table groaned under the weight of food.

Beral Babu, a lover of food and fish, had lost his appetite.

Binodini enjoyed the various dishes; she was just ravenous and with the attentive prince by her side, dinner was extremely enjoyable.

Lizzie ate like a horse and then continued her pursuit of the prince...who was as elusive as ever.

After dinner, they retired to the saloon. Beral Babu rushed and sat down next to Binodini even before the prince could attempt...and Lizzie who was waiting for such an opportunity sat close to her goal.

Black coffee with fresh cream was served in delicate gold-rimmed china cups.

"Let's turn in early, we have a busy day ahead," said the Maharani.

"The day will decide our fates Patta....I am worried...we have failed so many times before."

"I have a feeling we will see the light of day....end to all our troubles."

"I hope you are right."

Mishra hurried away; he had many arrangements to do.

As Binodini went into the bathroom to change into a thin cotton sari, Beral Babu stood watching the flames leaping in the fire.

11. Agni Pariksha

All these years, he had taken her for granted....now was he going to lose her....no, he would fight back....she was his...the love of his life.... he was going to win her back...shower her with love and attention.... which she would not be able to resist.

A knock on their door by the maid woke up Binodini....she hurriedly got dressed helped by the maid. Beral Babu teamed a white shirt with his black pant, and did his best to tease his hair to lie in a sleeker manner on his head.

Spraying a liberal amount of perfume on himself, he was ready. Binodini looked smart in a black woolen skirt teamed with a grey coat worn over a cream colour silk shirt.

"Wear this sweater or you will catch a cold," said Binodini.

"I am fine...even the prince does not wear sweaters," said Beral Babu a little grumpily.

Binodini went and hugged him and said, "I do not care about the prince."

The distance to the river was not much though it did necessitate a walk through the jungle, the prince had gone ahead on Nestor, Mishra as usual brought up the rear chatting with Beral Babu as they walked.... Lizzie was happily chatting with Binodini as if trying to make up for having ignored her the earlier evening, the doctor and his wife walked with the Maharaja and the Maharani....

Suddenly the Maharani, who was walking in between the doctor and his wife, uttered a loud shriek...all were shocked into silence... the Maharaja rushed to her side.

"Something bit me on the leg."

The doctor bent down and just next to her ankle a spot of blood was seen slowly spreading against the whiteness of her woolen pants.

"Snake bite…no doubt must have been a cobra."

The Maharani was slowly turning blue at the lips and she weakly sank to the ground, we have to take her back to the palace there is no time to be lost said the doctor as he cut open the wound area with a small penknife and started bleeding the wound.

Mishra had already harried a servant to inform the prince.

"She is losing consciousness… we cannot let that happen." The doctor kept the Maharani awake….all stood there helplessly watching unable to do much….Binodini clung to her husband crying and praying to god for help.

The prince arrived in a short while and Nestor was foaming furiously at the mouth. Picking up his mother he galloped to the palace followed by the doctor and the maharaja on horseback.

"Let's all hurry back," said Binodini and not even waiting to see if others were following suit, she walked and she ran, falling over difficult trails unmindful of the pain. Beral Babu and the others had a difficult time keeping up with her.

By the time Binodini and the others reached the palace, the Maharani had been already carried up to her ivory chambers, the doctor's wife hurried away to help her husband….the others waited outside the large teak door hoping and praying…it was almost an hour before the doctor opened the door.

Laying a hand on the Maharaja's shoulders, he said, "I have done everything that is humanely possible but I must also tell you that her body is almost paralysed from waist down and is turning blue. My treatment is unable to neutralise the effects of the poison, I have put her on drip…..pray hard that the poison does not reach her heart."

The Maharani lay inert on the silken covers of the large bed; her milky complexion had assumed a bluish shade and she looked so beautiful even in pain.

The doctor's wife who sat close by was crying softly.

Binodini watched in silence, her eyes floating in tears….the only thought that came to her mind at that moment was pray....pray asking God to help....

She left the Maharani's ivory chambers and rushed down the stairs, taking almost two at a time; at that moment of pain and despair the mandir was the only place that she could think off where there was still some hope of getting help.

She knelt on the cold floor in front of the statue of the mother Goddess and prayed, tears flowing down her eyes.... "Mother test not so take what you will from me...give her life....."

"My child may your prayer wrought the miracle.....the doctor but has a little hope.....we are doomed without our Maharani..." the calm and quiet voice belonged to the Raj Purohit....dressed in black with a red tilak on his forehead....his eyes hidden by his long flowing curly hair, he was a striking figure drawing both fear and respect...

"I will pray hard hoping against all odds....I wish I could do something....give my life for hers........."

Mishra was already there....waiting.... and hoping.

"Yes you can, madam....only you can if you want to save her," he said.

"Tell me what I can do....I will walk to the end of this Earth if I have to..." said Binodini.

"Raj Purohit knows...only he does...." said Mishra.

"Please tell me...." said Binodini tears flowing down her cheeks.

"If she is given a drink of water from the fountain of Gautama then she will live....."

"Where shall I find this fountain...?" asked Binodini.

"When a prince renounced this world, he sat under a Bodhi tree praying....the villagers would leave food for him....an old beggar women came to see this great soul....she had nothing to give....she left her begging bowl to him as a gift....the great soul used this very same bowl to eat and drink till he decided to leave this mortal body.... the bowl gave life to the dead....stolen and misused....it gives eternal life to the drinker and washes away all sins setting dammed souls free....there are many among us who tread this earth with immortal life.....the king of kings Asoka the great decided to safeguard the bowl from being misused by tyrants....guardians were appointed....our Maharaja is a descendent of these guardians...."

"If so then why the Maharaja is unable to help the Maharani....?" asked Binodini.

"Only a pure living mortal can touch the bowl and bring water from the fountain of Gautama...."

"Will you be my guide?" asked Binodini.

The Raj Purohit said nothing but beckoned her to follow him....they left the central courtyard of the palace and reached the grounds..... the sky had darkened with clouds and a cold wind had picked up pace.

Mishra knew the moment had come for which they had been waiting for....alert to any danger....he followed Binodini.

The two men sat outside the small thatched hut sharing a hookah... suddenly the bright sun disappeared under a blanket of clouds....cold winds howled down the mountain side....

"Let's go inside...I really have a bad feeling about all this."

"Just as father had described so many years ago....it is happening again...."

"What had happened...."

"Death of men, women and children....whole villages had death doing Tandav among the living."

The two men hurried into the hut calling out to their wives to bring the children inside.

The Raj Purohit stopped short in front of a tall wall of hedges.... "This is the maze, inside this in the centre you will find the fountain and the bowl of Gautama, I can only come this far; even Mishra cannot come with you....remember it won't be easy...you will face danger, have faith in God and yourself," he said.

Just near the entrance to the maze was a grave, inscribed on the gravestone were these words:

'Take the name of the mortal saint and he will clear your path of all evils'.

Binodini drew a deep breath and casting one last look at them both, she entered the maze.

"Pray this is last of our trials and tests...."

"My predictions if correct... our Maharani will be saved," said the Raj Purohit looking at Mishra.

Soon the tall hedges hid her from sight, she walked on the narrow path between the hedges and she looked up the only thing that she could see was the dark cloudy sky...the hedges widened leading to a square patch of grass and from each corner there was an exit as she stood there wandering which way to take.

"Look sisters, we have a visitor after so many years."

A startled Binodini turned around on hearing the voice...there stood three hooded figures.

The first crone who had spoken crackled and laughed loudly.

"Aha! A pretty one too," said the second crone.

"I can find many uses for such," said the third.

Binodini felt fear but she knew she had a life to save.

"Kind ones, can you please tell me which way to take," asked Binodini very humbly...

"She speaks well...hmmm," pointing to a large wooden chest that suddenly appeared near Binodini.

"Open that and take all your heart's content and leave before it is too late."

Binodini opened the large wooden chest...her eyes opened wide in amazement and surprise....jewels encrusted with precious gemstones like pearls, diamonds, rubies and emeralds. There were gold mohars and diamond tiaras...fit for a queen. Binodini closed the lid of the chest firmly.

"I desire not these; all I seek is the fountain and the bowl...please kind ones tell me which way to take," said Binodini.

"She is not like the other one sisters…we will tell you but first you have to answer a question from each of us…but be warned one wrong answer and you will be our slave for eternity to come."

"So be it," said Binodini.

"Which is the way to a man's heart?" asked the first.

"Through his stomach," answered Binodini…that was an easy one; she had always been advised so by her mother in law.

"How do you measure the air in your lungs?" asked the second.

Binodini thought for a while suddenly she remembered a game she played with her friends as a child…

"Sisters, she is silent…I knew she would fail….I will take her skin and wear it."

"Wait please…I shall tell…by the breath you take and the breath you miss, one feels the air as it fills yourself," said Binodini in one go.

"How did she know that…she is sharp…make the third a difficult venture," said the second crone.

"I walk with you, I run and sleep with you, there is no you without me, when you get wet I am twig dry…what am I?"

Binodini pondered a while than very calmly replied, "Shadow."

The three crones howled, driving fear into Binodini's heart but she stood her ground "Which way to take?" she asked firmly.

A bony hand with sharp claw like nails pointed her the way.

She walked for quite some time the day seemed like night, worried what she would find ahead of her….the maze took twists and turns she kept a sharp lookout as she walked….there were just tall walls of green ivy and the dark stormy sky above. The maze suddenly opened up into a small grass clearing.

There were three women, hideous creatures squabbling and quarrelling among themselves….they were frightful looking with sharp teeth protruding out…no eyes or lips…skin like that of a snake, wearing nothing but bits and pieces of skin…they were more animal than human.

"Give me that it is mine…I took it out from the last one."

"No I will not I too shall wear."

"Why you only…if I do not get it I will tear your eyes out"

The other two crackled and laughed….

"We have no eyes, you fool."

Binodini saw a large eyeball lying on the grass the eye was alive and was looking this way and that way, seeing Binodini it fixed its sharp gaze on her…

"I smell human."

"Me too."

"Me also."

"OOOHOOO! EYES where are you, come to mother."

The eyes darted off to the caller who picked it up and wore it on her forehead…the other two who were blind clung to each other for support.

"A beautiful human female…what nice eyes you have, that too two of them."

"What two eyes, I want one," said one.

"One for me too," said the second.

The one with the eye came close to her and sniffed her with her beak like nose and then she spoke her voice ringing loud and clear.

"What is your quest we know?

 Further you can go if you play.

Without delay.

A game with us.

Without creating a fuss.

Lose you will.

Pay us with your eye.

Without a sigh…

Win you reach.

Without a breach."

Binodini thought for but just a moment and said…..

"Play I will and win I will.

State what you have in mind.

So that I can bind."

The one-eyed woman pointed her long bony fingers at the grass and lo! there appeared square tiles; floating above each tile were little figures as if alive—some had horses rearing and neighing while on some there were birds flying. Still others had dragons breathing fire and fishes swimming in the air. The tiles realigned themselves on the ground and formed a game of hopscotch.

"Remember and be warned play well, step with God's name," said the crone.

"Here take the golden dice, fall it should without a vice," said the second.

Taking a deep breath, Binodini looked at the spread of the game… the moment she tried to take a step the figures of birds and animals turned alert and watching, where to step and throw her dice she wandered. Taking God's name…was what the one eyed crone had said. Among all the figures there was none depicting any God…then the story about the mortal saint came to her mind…as a child her father would often read out to her about one such mortal saint who sat under a tree on a seat of lotus, of course that was it…now she knew where to step for among the tiles were the ones with tiny floating lotus flowers whose petals closed and opened. At the end of the row there was just but one single tile with a pair of feet that were walking round and round in circles. She threw the golden dice at the feet of the mortal saint and jumped and stepped only on those tiles having the tiny lotus flowers whose petals closed tightly as she steeped on them. In no time she completed the game without making a single mistake….as a child back in her village there was none who could beat her in the game of hop scotch….these old crones were no match for her.

"Now that I have completed the game, show me the path to take," asked Binodini.

"She wants to go."

"What about her eyes?"

The one with the eye spoke "Now, now where is the hurry? Play with us some more, we will tell you the way then."

Binodini sensed danger as all the three guided by the sighted one started coming closer to her.

"Yes I would love to play but first let us decide to whom shall I give my eyes to...I personally feel only the prettiest among you should get my beautiful eyes," said Binodini.

"Only she can see for she always keeps the eye... how to decide who is the prettiest? Asked one among them."

"Take it from her as she is not very fair with you both and you two being much prettier than her," said Binodini cunningly.

A fight broke out the sighted one was no match for the other two. One among them dug out the eye from the sighted ones face, this was the opportunity Binodini was waiting for and she snatched the eye from the bony fingers and moved away to a safe distance....

"She has tricked us."

"Catch her."

"I will rip her skin off and wear it."

"Do not try anymore or I shall squash the eye under my boots," Binodini said angrily.

"No please do not so."

"Tell her the way."

"If you do not I shall."

The three raised their claw like fingers and chanted.

Go not east, go not west.

Come to me for I know the best.

Hailstorm, thunder, lightning, bolt.

Fall where you must.

Do not be a dolt.

A sharp stinging bolt of light fell with a loud crackle on the formidable green wall of ivy and lo! a path opened for Binodini to take.

She threw the eye into a far corner and took the path in a run.

"It has been quite some time now....I feel waiting is futile... let us inform the Maharaja we are doomed," said Mishra seeing the delay.

"No Patta Nath, wait.... be patient, you young people lack wisdom; our pains and trials are about to end I can feel it" said the Raj Purohit laying a restraining hand on his shoulder.

Binodini at last reached the centre of the maze and here the grass was green, soft moss like in which her boots sank deep as she walked. Suddenly somebody spoke behind her startling her....

"I have been waiting for you a very long time. I was told one would come who would release me from this curse."

A warrior in armour stood tall before her, he was young and very handsome.

"I seek not a fight soldier; all I want is the bowl and water from the fountain of Gautama," said Binodini.

"It is not in my hands to give or take; I am but just a guardian," he said.

"Please than guide me to it for a life depends on it," pleaded Binodini.

"Come with me I shall lead you to...but the choice is yours," he said.

He drew his sword and thrust it with full force into the bosom of the mother Earth....the mouth of a cave opened leading deep into the depths of hell. Beckoning her to follow he lead the way, he took so many turns and corners that soon Binodini lost count, the ceiling was low and the path narrow she crawled after the warrior to reach a large cavern...there was no light here, yet Binodini could see as clear as day, the walls of the cave twinkled as if with a thousand stars, in the centre of the cave was a fountain bubbling with water as green as emerald.

The warrior pointed to an array of bowls of all sizes and shapes kept on shelves carved out in the walls of the cave.

"Choose wisely my lady for a wrong choice will…." He trailed off into a silence pointing to many mummified figures lying heaped in a corner of the cave.

Some were large, some were small, fit for a king they were all. She looked wandering which could be it, would it be the one with diamonds, emeralds and rubies set in gold or would it be the one in silver set with pearls. Then she remembered the story the Raj Purohit had told her….a beggar woman's begging bowl…in one corner towards the very end of the row Binodini found what she thought should be it.

"If you think it so than let it be so," said the warrior.

Binodini filled the bowl with water from the fountain and as she turned to leave….

"Better to check what you have chosen that is the law of reason," he said.

"I have no time for that…as it is I am late, please I should leave…" she said.

"I cannot allow you to leave until you do the bidding….I am sorry but these are my orders."

Binodini had but no choice she raised the bowl and drank it all, the water was cold as ice, such….which she had never ever tasted.

"Wise choice I must say, come fill it up and I shall be your guide all the way," he said.

They went on harried foot towards the exit of the maze…Binodini held the bowl careful so as not to spill a drop of water.

"This is as far as I go," said he and left.

"Thank god here she comes," said the Raj Purohit.

"Give it to me, we have no time to lose," said Mishra.

Taking it from her outstretched hands, he hurried away to the palace, followed by a very weary and tired Binodini at a much slower pace, the Raj Purohit walked by her side alert to any danger.

The two men huddled in front of a small fire spoke in hushed tones.

"I pray to God to save us, it seems as if the heavens are angry look how ominously dark the skies have turned."

"I too feel the same....wonder what is in store for us."

They shared a hookah and looked glumly at each other.

"Where is Binodini? I cannot find her anywhere, have you seen her?" asked a very worried and distraught looking Beral Babu to Mishra.

"Please do not be worried, we all were at the temple praying...she is on her way with the Raj Purohit."

"Before we go in there...I need to ask something of you my child..." said the Raj Purohit to her.

"Did you drink...?"

Binodini remained silent, a look of helpless guilt writ on her face.

"Speak not of today...to anyone ever....not to him also, it is for your own safety and his," said the Raj Purohit with very serious look on his face.

Beral Babu was waiting for her on the steps, as they reached the portico, seeing her he came down the remaining steps in a mad rush and took her in his arms.

"I was so worried...." he said. She clung to the warm safety, her heart heavy that she could never ever tell him.

"She has saved us all, you chose well this time Patta....but...the serious accident could have been avoided," the Maharaja said with a bit of worry and sadness.

"Could do worse....he would have come too.... she will come through...I have found out," he continued with his head bowed with respect.

"There is still a lot left in the bowl," said Mishra.

"Pour it into the fountain in the central courtyard and we all shall drink and cleanse our dammed souls tonight," said the Maharaja with a smile.

They were all in the saloon....waiting for doctor. It was a while before he walked in with a large smile writ on his face..... "Binodini's prayers have been answered....she is saved."

"Can I see her...?" asked Binodini.

The beautiful Maharani of Darimbari was sleeping peacefully.

"Calls for a celebration, Patta; make arrangements. We will be celebrating the pujo here in the Palace, that is what Binodini wishes, then so shall it be kept," said the Maharaja with a large smile of happiness on his face.

The prince came very close to her as she stood next to Beral Babu, and taking her hands in his he said "A true warrior princess indeed...a savior of us all I can never thank you enough."

Beral Babu laid a possessive arm around Binodini's shoulders... the prince noticed it and smiled knowingly....he bowed very gallantly and moved away.

That night, there was special celebration in the palace, dancers and singers had been called and the merry making continued all night, dinner was a lavish affair and served in the central courtyard, all the palace staff, servants and soldiers came to share their Maharaja's happiness. Much later, after everyone had left, a large bonfire was lit around which they sat and raised a toast to the Maharani's health.... of course Mishra had to be there with his brand of scary stories to frighten Beral Babu. One could feel the cheer in every soul who lived in the palace.

All were sleeping inside the small hut huddled close together to keep out the cold, the small fire in the make shift kitchen had long died out, even there were no glowing embers left to lend any heat to the room.

One of the men woke up shivering, he was really having bad dreams these days....could his forefathers find no other place to work or serve. He tried to relight the fire cursing the heavens for his state.

"What are you doing, you dimwit....scaring me like that in the middle of the night I thought a wolf had broken in.....if you had not

been married to my sister I would have wrung your scrawny neck with my bare hands," said other man who had woken up hearing the sounds in the kitchen.

Seeing his futile attempts to light the fire he pushed the other man away "move let me do that, all that soft living in the palace has spoilt you totally....no embers... how do you expect to light this? You ass....go get some embers from the mandir, they always keep a fire on there.... especially on such nights as this."

The skies over laden with clouds, as if it would pour at any moment, though the winds had died down yet the cold had become unbearable seeping into every pore in one's body.

"Give me that iron plate; I will go and get some live embers." As he opened the door and stepped out, the howling was heard loud and clear.

"Come inside you fool....can you not hear that... seems like a whole pack, you will get us all killed."

"When my father was alive he would speak of....a pack of wolves that chased him in these very same jungles." Hurriedly they closed the door, better to be cold than dead. The howling continued deep into the night and it kept both men awake and alert.

12. Elder Prince

Tired yet happy, all called it a night. Hand in hand the couple walked upstairs, the prince watched them and felt happy...Lizzie came and stood next to him.

"You love her, don't you?"

The prince smiled and walked away leaving her to ponder.

As Binodini changed in the bathroom, her thoughts raced to the day's events....she must have dreamt all that....if she told any of this to her friends they would think of her as a raving lunatic....might be it was all a dream.

"We have overslept, get up sleepy head," Beral Babu shook Binodini gently.

Everyone had almost finished their breakfast when Binodini and Beral Babu reached the dining hall. After breakfast, the doctor and his wife took their leave and left for their home in the hills. The Maharaja and the Maharani saw off their guests, Lizzie threw a kiss at the prince then rode off on her dun colour mare. The Maharaja and Mishra having gone to settle a state matter, the three decided to spend a lazy day in the lawns playing croquet.

"I am feeling so exhausted....let us sit down," said the Maharani with a laugh.

"Do not exert yourself so....you should rest, the doctor said the poison was extremely toxic," said Binodini.

The Maharani took her hands in her own and looked deep into her eyes.

"I do not know how to thank you enough for saving my life," said she.

Beral Babu, who was listening to all this said, "Give her your blessings; that is all we need."

There was a weak sun in the sky…a cold morning, yet sitting outside sipping cups of hot ginger flavoured tea and keeping one's feet warm by the sigdi that Gobordhan had placed strategically, one near every chair…. the situation was not all unpleasant, Beral Babu closed his eyes and dozed off. Binodini was reminded of the cold winter mornings when she was a small girl…the kitchen used to be outside in the courtyard, her mother would light the chullah to cook breakfast for them and Binodini would sit close to her hiding her face in her bosom soaking in the warmth of her mother's love and affection. Her mother died young just a year after her marriage….she missed her so much.

Almost reading her thoughts, the Maharani said, "Learn to live on your own terms, we miss those who leave us, but that does not mean we should stop loving ourselves for what we are worth…..as you judge yourself, so will others judge you."

Just then Gobordhan came and stood in front of the Maharani…. trying to catch his breath he spoke.

"Seek to speak to Hujoor….Khan has come with news about the elder prince."

"Where is he? Bring him to me at once…."

Gobordhan ran back the way he had come.

"Let us go back to the Palace as we cannot speak of this here."

They all got up and hurried back to the palace. Khan was waiting for the Maharani in the large hall. Seeing her he bowed low and folded his hands with respect.

"I have not failed this time, but we have to hurry."

"I shall leave at once then," said the prince…asking Gobordhan to saddle up Nestor.

With Maharaja and Mishra away…she was worried, she had already known great pain on account of the elder prince, just Khan alone was not enough to protect the prince on a path fraught with great dangers.

Beral Babu looked at the worried face of the Maharani as she stood on the tiger skin looking at the flames leaping in the fire place. He knew she was worrying about the prince's safety.

"Do not worry so....I will also go with him."

"No you must not, there is great danger and you are not a man of war, if anything happens...."

"I am not afraid to face danger....do not worry."

As Beral Babu pulled on a heavy sweater over his shirt, Binodini came and stood in front of him. She was afraid and did not want him to go.

"With the Maharaja away, I feel it is my duty to go with him, if you still feel I should not than I shall not...." saying this Beral Babu waited near the door.

"Here take this monkey cap; your ears are sensitive to cold," said Binodini.

In the central courtyard, the prince was waiting with Khan.

"Have you filled the silver flask with water from the fountain and the bowl? Keep them both safely."

"My prince, do you think we should take him with us?"

"The Raj Purohit feels otherwise; I share the same concerns as you Khan."

"Be quiet, here he comes, protect him at all costs if need arises," said the prince quietly in Khan's ears.

Khan led the way on a large grey stallion followed by the prince on Nestor with Beral Babu sitting behind him on the double saddle. They were quite a sight....Khan wrapped in a blanket, the dashing prince in his plumed helmet and Beral Babu in his monkey cap clinging to the prince for his dear life as they galloped away.

The two men were walking back from the small post office near the mandir, just a one roomed makeshift arrangement in which the postmaster slept, eat and worked too. On seeing these two, he seemed annoyed, almost every day they would turn up in the morning when he was the busiest as usual inquiring about any letter or telegram, today he shooed them off saying....

"Yes I am sure queen Victoria will write to you soon...but for now get lost before I call the constable."

"What my sister saw in you I do not know, if I would have been married to you, I would have wrung your scrawny neck with my bare hands.....today just for you I got insulted by that old frog."

"I have my responsibilities....."

"Yes I am sure you do......but to others, what about my sister... you ass!"

One grumbling about his sister's biggest mistake in life and the other wandering, the two men hurried back home.

The horses galloped fast and furious, Beral Babu who had never ever sat on anything faster than his scooter, clung tightly to the prince and kept his eyes shut, each time Nestor jumped over fallen trees or galloped downhill, Beral Babu had a strong feeling that this was his last day on mother Earth. The grasslands and sand beds of the river soon gave away to rocky and hilly terrain, the horses were extremely surefooted and made good speed even on such difficult grounds. They stopped only when they reached an impenetrable wall of jungle.

"We have to go by foot from here," said Khan.

"What about the horses?" asked the prince.

A little ahead near a stream Rishi kasha Darpana had made his ashram. The ashram consisted of a few huts and sheds made out of bamboo and jungle grass.

The Rishi was a very wise man with long flowing white hair that swept the ground as he walked, his beard must have been long too for it was knotted at three places to keep it out of his way. As they walked into the ashram they could see a few disciples under a thatched shed who were seating on asanas made out of leaf and studying ancient manuscripts, while the Rishi sat on a platform covered with a tiger skin.

While Khan tied the horses, the prince followed by Beral Babu approached the Rishi with folded hands, the Rishi had striking white bushy eyebrows over a pair of deep dark eyes. Seeing them approach, he simply closed his eyes and went into a trance. Khan joined them after having watered and tethered the horses.

"I have been waiting...it was about time," said the Rishi with his eyes still closed.

"Seek your permission to leave our horses here, the jungle we shall have to cover by foot," said the prince.

"What you are seeking I know off....but your path is difficult and full of danger," said the Rishi.

"Mahatman we have but very little time....please take care of my friend here for I will be leaving him behind in your care," said the prince pointing at Beral Babu in a monkey cap.

The Rishi rose from his seat and beckoned them to follow him and at a short distance from the shed was a small thatched hut. Asking them to wait, he went inside. When he came out he held a small potli.

"I have been asked to give this to you....here take," he came close to a very surprised Beral Babu and thrust it into his hands.

Beral Babu opened the potli....in it was a small twig. As he took it out, to his horror it looked more like a dried human finger with the nail still attached to it.

"What is this?.....it looks like...." said Beral Babu.

The Rishi just smiled and nodded, Beral Babu uttered a cry and dropped it.

"What on Earth do you think you are doing.....you will get us all killed," shouted the Rishi.

The prince quickly picked up the human finger from the ground and put it back in the potli.

"How am I to use this?" asked the prince.

"Not you....him," said the Rishi pointing to Beral Babu.

"A very shocked Beral Babu asked, "what am I going to do with it?.......tickle somebody?"

"If that is what you want to," smiled the Rishi mischievously.

"It is a dangerous path fraught with many dangers…he won't be safe…..he is not the fighting material…..." the prince trailed into a silence.

"Without his kind of valor by your side you stand to lose all, my prince." Saying this, the Rishi walked away.

Khan cleared a path cutting through vines, creepers and overhanging branches, the under growth was thick and it made going very difficult. Beral Babu walked in-between them, unaccustomed to any kind of physical exertion. He was soon out of breath; his heavy breathing could be heard loud and clear in the stillness of the jungle……

"Huzjoor, it is too quiet…." said Khan alert as ever.

Both of them drew their swords, Beral Babu wondered if he was to draw out the human finger from the potli.

A soft rustling was heard in the over growth….a slight bending of grass blades…..khan's trained senses missed nothing, then came the attack and it came from all sides, it was sudden and swift, the jungle resounded with horrifying howls and angry growls, for Beral Babu who had never ever faced anything more terrifying then the mongrels near his house this was like a horrifying dream with no escape. Khan and the prince shielded him and fought back as best as they could, steel against flesh.

Teeth tearing at human soul terrified Beral Babu out of his wits, backing against a large tree, he crouched down hopping to escape the onslaught but a large lone wolf was watching his every move. Back arched, eyes glowing coal red and fangs dripping saliva the beast came at him, he called for help but both Khan and the prince were themselves under heavy attack….he picked up a thick branch from the forest floor and fought back….the jungle resounded with growls, and Beral Babu's howls.

The prince had seen the peril that Beral Babu was facing with just a stick in hand…..a brave man indeed….with one swing of his sword he killed the beast, with the leader of the pack dead, the rest fled into the deeper parts of the forest. Heavily wounded the three sat against the bole of a large tree…..the wounds and claw marks of the other two healed within seconds…..

"Come… let us move we have no time to waste," said the prince.

"Hujoor, his wounds are deep….he is bleeding heavily from his neck," said Khan as he wrapped his muffler around trying to stop the bleeding.

"Use some of your jungle medicine…..here take my scarf….it would have been better if he would have stayed back in the ashram," said the prince a little worried.

"The beast got the artery I think…..I am unable to stop the blood….like this he will die within minutes," said Khan.

The prince stood helpless…..Binodini's face floated in front of his eyes, after all that she has done for them….he owed it to her.

"Give me the flask." Pouring some water into the bowl he held it to Beral Babu's lips.

"What happened to me…why is my sweater soaked in blood?" Beral Babu looked like a man who had just got up from a deep sleep.

"Nothing, you got knocked up in the head, here let me take back my muffler," said Khan.

They moved through the forest alert, the heavy stillness of the jungle broken by yelps and curses from Beral Babu who often slipped and fell or got caught in the face with over hanging branches of trees, they followed the stream that was fed with water from the melting ice.

At places, they crossed the stream and Beral Babu found the going very difficult, cursing every drop of water that fed the stream he clung tightly to Khan's brawny arms for support.

Khan pointed to the mouth of a cave high up on the mountain side, it was almost invisible due to the thick under growth and over hanging branches and vines, they crept towards the mouth of the cave, Beral Babu stayed behind as a lookout whereas the other two entered cautiously.

Outside the cave, Beral Babu could hear the thick buzzing sound of the insects that lived in the bark of the pine and fir trees. The air was cold and damp. Beral Babu had the most unsettling feeling of being watched.

He backed into a tree and sat down on his hunches; it had been quite some time now since the prince and Khan had gone into the cave, he heard a low growl coming from within him, his stomach was really making its presence felt, he regretted not having taken up Gobordhan's offer of halwa and puris, just some fruits and a glass of milk was not his idea of starting the day. Suddenly he heard a loud rustling in the bushes behind him, with his heart in his mouth he looked around for a suitable weapon to defend himself, not a stick or stone in sight. The prince and khan being away he did not know what he should do?, he pressed himself closer to the bole of the tree, he heard the rustling slowly closing on him....he suddenly remembered the potli in his pant pocket....knowing that it was a mad idea, still he thought it is better to have a 'blind uncle' than none at all.

He took it out and held it tightly between his fingers as if it was some kind of a sword....

"What are you doing here my son, in this part of the jungle where men fear to tread?"

Beral Babu had expected to be attacked by a fierce animal from behind the tall grass but before him stood an old woman dressed in odd bits of skin. She held a small basket in one hand and a large stick in the other to support herself. Seeing her ,Beral Babu hid the dried human finger in his palm and got up from his awkward position. What a relief he felt on seeing another human being.

"My friends are inside....I am the lookout, anyway as for you, you are too old to be out on your own," said he.

The old woman crackled and laughed showing toothless black gums.

"What about you? Are you not too fat and soft to be out alone?" said she.

Beral Babu had heard enough of fat jokes his whole life and this brand of humour from an old woman was totally indigestible.

"I will refrain from making such jokes if I was you….me and anger are like peas of the same pod."

"Is it?" the old woman hitting him hard with her stick.

The stick found its mark and he started bleeding furiously from his temple.

"What are you mad….why are hitting me?" The pain was too much Beral Babu howled in horror.

At the sight of blood the old woman licked her lips hungrily… it was long since she had fed decently.

"I am so sorry I did not mean to do that…..come son let me look at that wound," said she with a great show of sympathy.

Making Beral Babu sit on a rock, she wiped the wound with a piece of jungle moss….

"What in God's name….are you licking my wound?" A shocked Beral Babu jumped away from the old woman, she stood there looking at him, watching, and waiting.

"We have not fed decently for a very long time," her voice almost a whisper.

Beral Babu, until now, had only dealt with the likes of Rangamashi and this was way over his head.

She had said 'we' that meant there were others, this was just an old woman with a taste for blood….if he could find something to defend himself with. Unfortunately, she had backed him up against the mouth of the cave, it was too dark for his liking, he knew she was going to attack…..she looked extremely threatening. She lunged at him her bony fingers clawing at his face, somehow Beral Babu managed to push her back. She surprisingly possessed great strength and at once she was back taking another lunge at him, she tried to bite where she could, Beral Babu yelped in pain, his cry set off a kind of feeding frenzy in her, she now tried to tear at his flesh instead of just biting, he fell backwards and she was at once upon him, in his hand he was still holding what the Rishi had given him....tickle he had said....he pocked her in the ribs with it....as hard as he could, a glowing red hot light passed through the fiend burning her to cinders within seconds.

Beral Babu was too shocked to understand what had happened but he knew that what the Rishi had given him, was indeed a formidable weapon of death. He stood up hesitatingly expecting pain and hurt but surprisingly he felt none; he touched his temple gingerly the skin had healed and there was no pain at all, he was a bit bewildered.

The old woman had spoken about others....he was no brave a soldier to face a few others like her. Instead, he thought of going in search of the other two... the sooner he found them the quicker he could leave and return to his Binodini. Holding his newfound weapon firmly in his hand, ready to jab anyone who dare come near, he entered the cave. It was absolutely pitch black, undecided he stood not knowing what to do, just then from the tip of the finger arose a red glow that changed into bright white light lighting up the cave.

The floor of the cave slanted downwards and it widened into a large number of tunnels and caverns, it was difficult to guess which way the others had gone. Beral Babu stood biting his lower lips wandering.... long back during his college days he had seen an English talkie where the hero followed and caught the badie by following his footsteps in the sand.....he looked at the cave floor. There were indeed a pair of human footprints crisscrossed by animal prints seemed like dogs or most probably wolves.

He followed the footprints deep into the very hellish depths of the cave.

"What light is that Narka?" asked the brutish looking, tall figure that stood hidden behind a jutting wall of the cave.

"I do not know my Lord but the light is very hot and burnt down two of our guards who had gone to stop it from advancing."

"You take ten of our best and stop that thing from coming any further," said the Lord of the Asuras.

Narka was afraid yet he had no choice, either die a hellish death at the hands of their brutish ruler or get burnt by this strange light.....

Warriors from the depths came and attacked they crept, jumped and lunged....only thing that remained of these were smoke and dust...the hot burning light kept advancing, Beral Babu unaware of the existence of any other life forms followed the foot prints keeping a sharp look out for wolves.

"Where is Narka?"

"He is no more, my Lord," replied the second in command.

The fangs drew back in an angry grimace....eyes glowing like red-hot coals, the ruler was furious every one feared this mood of his.

Beral Babu had now reached a large cavern and was horrified to see the floor littered with bones and skulls of humans and animals.

He felt worried about the prince and Khan...most probably meal by now to whatever that lived in these caves. The roof was high and it seemed as if there were nests of some kind in the walls.

Carrying large rocks the size of boulders they renewed the attack, they threw the boulders from the top....from the sides but to no avail each time they melted down to sand and dust.

Though he could see clearly yet suddenly the cavern had turned dusty and Beral Babu, who was extremely allergic, started coughing and sneezing.

The ruler kept a safe distance from the searing heat of the light, he could sniff human flesh but approaching the light meant death.

"What happened to Surakha?"

"Why did she not stop the human outside?"

The second in command thought better not to give an answer to that. Beral Babu raised his hand higher trying to see what was there in those nests above him, the effect of his action was catastrophic…… cinder and ash flew all over the place….Beral Babu could take it no more he kept sneezing, he moved on to the next adjoining caves, where ever he went dust, cinder and ash flew in thick clouds. Coughing, sneezing and wheezing he kept searching for the others.

"My lord, he has destroyed the nests and most of our strength… still he is heading further into our flanks…unstoppable power."

"Where is he heading to now?" asked the mighty lord of the Asuras.

"He has reached the inner sanctums….the harem is threatened."

"Tell the suraruni's to flee….at once."

The second in command at once send a messenger to warn the queen and the other suraruni's. Beral Babu looked at the walls of the cave which glittered with a thousand lights, going close he dug with his finger nail and an egg-sized rock emitting white fire fell out; thinking it would be a nice gift for Binodini, he dug out quite a few of them and kept them in his pockets, as he was busy so was the messenger who was trying to creep past him but unfortunately at that very appointed moment he dropped a small rock that was emitting red glow so he bent down to pick it up, coughing and sneezing Beral Babu stood up thinking what a disgusting dusty place it was. He continued raising more dust and cinders…..still he could find sign no sign of the other two.

"He has destroyed the harem, my lord," a very fearful second in command stood before the towering figure of the Asura king. The king was furious yet helpless, unable to wreck his vengeance.

"I feel he is searching for something, my lord," said the second in command.

"No….he is looking for our captives."

"Lead him to them than we can capture him easily….the other

two cannot be made meal off, they simply refuse to die but this one I am sure is different."

Beral Babu was not only feeling tired but also hunger and thirst was driving him crazy, he heard the sound of gurgling water not very far from where he stood, he decided to give one last try….the cavern was much wider and bigger than the previous one, in the centre was a large fountain like structure hewn out of rock and cold water flowed down that ran into a deep underground cavern, so far so good he had seen no threat to his safety, for a minute he thought of keeping it in his pocket and drinking to his fill, but in creepy places such as these often our own sense plays havoc with us, Beral Babu had the most creepiest feeling of someone looking down at him; he also thought he heard a low growl. Afraid, he again lifted his hand focusing the bright light on the high walls of the cave, dust and cinders rose in unison as he moved his hand.

The king lay prone behind a large rock, burnt yet alive, trying not to make a single sound as that would attract the searing light towards himself, the whole of his pack had been destroyed and the curse of the Rishi had come true…..the warrior had indeed come and he had failed to save his clan.

A loud groan escaped Khan's lips as his severed limbs started growing back….the prince lay inert on a large slab of rock. It was some time before he could reach the prince's side; keeping an eye open for the beasts, he waited for the prince to heal.

"Where are the silver flask and the bowl, Khan? Before they come back, let us rescue the elder prince," said the prince who looked as if he had just woken up from a very deep sleep.

Khan was clever; when the attack happened he had hidden his bag under a jutting rock. The two men hurried through the narrow passage to reach the cave, which had a fountain with gurgling cold water that flowed into an underground cavern.

They groped their way through pitch-black darkness when suddenly at the end of the long narrow passage they saw bright light, they hurried towards it and to their surprise they found Beral Babu standing near the fountain drinking water with one cupped palm while in the other he held what the Rishi had given to him.

"Did you not see them....I am so glad to see you safe and in one piece," said the prince.

"I saw nothing but for an old woman who wanted to eat me, these caves are so dusty, I have been sneezing and coughing throughout, very dirty and smelly too wander what kind of animals ever lived here," said a very happy Beral Babu who felt glad to have found the other two safe.

"Come let us move quickly, my prince, we cannot risk another attack," said the alert Khan with his sword drawn.

The trio moved quickly, Khan knew where the elder prince was. The tunnel became narrower until the three were crawling on their hands and knees. The tunnel opened into a small cave, the narrow uneven steps lead down to a small platform made out of a large slab of rock. Khan and the prince put their shoulders against the lid and shoved as hard as they could, it would not budge an inch....after a few futile attempts, they gave up knowing it was hopeless, by the time they could bring back help, the beasts would shift the prince somewhere else and this meant another search lasting an eternity.

Beral Babu looked at both of them; he knew he would not be of much help but still another try with him pitching in would be of no harm. Reluctant at first but with a little persuasion from Beral Babu the two agreed. The other two laid their shoulders against the slab and shoved with all their might while Beral Babu pushed with one hand, logic behind his doing so was who would hold the light otherwise. The slab shifted and fell off to one side revealing a flight of narrow uneven steps; a very quiet Khan and a very bewildered prince shook their heads in wonder. It was decided that Beral Babu would stand guard while the other two would go down, Khan kept lighting the mashals on the walls as they made their way downstairs.

Unknown to the three, a lone figure had crawled after them, it lay behind a rock away from the reach of the bright light, watching and waiting. Its burnt body raw red and its limbs twisted but the face had remained unscathed and in its glowing red hot eyes there was vengeance and mad rage.

The steps suddenly ended and widened into a very small cave with very low roof, both being tall of height bent low and moved near to a small cage, the irons bars had turned rusty with age, through the bars a small mummified hand of a child hung out as if making a last plea for help....tears welled up in the prince's eyes seeing how helpless his brother had been in his death.

Quickly Khan poured water from the silver flask into the bowl and handed it to the prince; then using all his brute strength he pried open the door of the cage, the small figure of a boy revealed itself as Khan gently removed him and laid him on the floor of the cave, the prince very carefully poured the water on the lips of the figure that were dry and closed. He sprinkled some on the figure too just as the Raj Purohit had instructed. Lo! Behold miracle happened before their own eyes.....the body regenerated itself skin, bone, flesh and sinew formed anew, the elder prince woke up as if from a deep slumber.

Beral Babu was surprised to see the elder prince, a little boy of seven, he expected someone more mature and older, the prince was weak and was carried carefully by Khan wrapped in his blanket, looking at Khan...Beral Babu thought how odd he looked just like a hen with its feathers plucked out.

The three made their way out of the cave, the feel of fresh mountain air and the daylight was a relief from the oppressive atmosphere of the cave. Unaware of the figure that watched them go with the knowledge that they had something that would bring back the dead and the figure knew that his turn too would come.

The Rishi was waiting for them.....

Beral Babu walked up to the Rishi, handed him back the potli, and thanked him profusely. "The light it emitted helped me to see in the dark cave."

"I am sure it did, do you not need it anymore?" asked the Rishi with a knowing smile.

"No I am sure I do not need it….for I am never going to venture into such dark places again," said Beral Babu very confidently.

"In case you do I am sure you know where to find it," saying this the Rishi moved away to make arrangements for his guests' night stay.

Early next morning, they left…Beral Babu riding pillion behind the prince wearing his monkey cap, khan carefully carried the elder prince wrapped in a blanket, they went slow and steady….there was no more hurry their search had ended.

The sun was but an orange glow when they reached the palace. Everyone was waiting in the central courtyard for their prince who had come back a victor. The Maharaja and Maharani took their son and held him close. They had lost him so many years ago now he was back. They thanked Beral Babu for his bravery, Binodini stood there proud of her husband's deeds.

"I need a hot bath, the caves were so dusty and dirty and I sneezed and coughed the whole time….look in my pant pockets I have got something for you."

Binodini halted the maid and checked his pockets; indeed, he had brought back something for her…the stones were shiny and looked lovely against the light. "I like these from where did you find so many of them…I think once we go back I will buy a fish tank and put these in it, it will look lovely," she said very happily.

That night it seemed as if the whole palace was alive and celebrating, everywhere one went the sound of joy and laughter was heard. The bells of the mandir kept chiming celebrating the release of the elder prince.

Dinner was a very lavish affair; the Maharani had herself

overseen the dishes, a very famished Beral Babu eat his fill. While others sat down to chat over a cup of coffee in the saloon, he snored softly in one corner of the sofa. It was much later that Khan carried him upstairs.

Before leaving he turned towards Binodini and said, "Very brave man.....I am proud to make acquaintance of such a brave soul."

As per the Maharaja's orders, Mishra doubled the guards in the palace and also asked Khan to keep an eye open for any threat.

The elder prince was treated by the palace vaid; he was not only weak in body but the Maharani was also worried about the wounds that his soul had suffered at the hands of his abductors. The little boy was fearful of new faces and stayed in his room most of the time. Slowly but surely he recovered; the Maharaja and the Maharani's happiness knew no bounds as the young prince soon become his old cheerful self. The little boy could be heard playing around in the palace. Mishra and Khan both kept a vigilant eye, Beral Babu with his first experience on the horse suffered a bad back and raw knees quite happily for Binodini never left his side and at his first groan would rub his back and soothe his pain.

As they sat down to a quiet lunch, Gobordhan hurried in with a telegram, the Maharaja skimmed through it.

"Your brother is reaching here from Bristol in the evening," he said with a naughty twinkle in his eyes.

"Now do not give me that look....I never say anything when your sister comes to town," said Maharani with a wicked grin.

"Oh that reminds me my sister will be coming too, to attend the pujo celebration at the palace," he said grinning wider.

"Really how very forgetful not to have told me that earlier?" said the Maharani.

Binodini loved their show of sweet and sour love, the beautiful Maharani of Darimbari really had her man under loving finger tips.

Gobordhan was summoned and asked to make arrangements for their stay.

Mishra was asked to ensure that their rooms were in two opposite directions of the cupids.

13. A Very Bristol Gentleman

Before the cock could doodle and the sun could rise, a loud angry voice from under her window woke up Binodini.

"Dare you ask for two annas from the queen's brother after all that I had to endure at the hands of you and your donkey," the voice shouted at the top of his throat.

Binodini looked down; all she could see were two floppy ears and a large furry face that was making good use of the queen's hedges. She realised that their guest who was supposed to come a day earlier had at last arrived. She hurried to wake up her husband but his side of the bed was empty, wandering where he had gone to she hurried to the bathroom.

Binodini hurried to the dining hall, at such an early hour in the morning she found the Maharani pouring hot cups of tea for Beral Babu and another gentleman who she assumed must be the queen's brother. On seeing her, the Maharani called her over to join them.

"With the prince away, I have to thank your husband for receiving my brother at the station at this unearthly hour....come let me introduce you to him," said she.

The Maharani's brother, all of fifty years with a receding hairline, was extremely well endowed and it seemed the line gravity had a difficult time deciding where to pass through because his thin shapely legs were very unsuited for such punishment. His owl-like eyes set under thick bushy eyebrows scrutinized Binodini very closely, his teeth were large and very white as he got up from his seat and came close to her and smiled, his large droopy moustache gave him an appearance of a beached walrus, altogether not bad at all for a man of law, practicing in Bristol.

"Aha! I am glad to make acquaintance of you young lady; my name is Shekhar, I know yours and my sister speaks very high of you. I am eternally grateful to you for saving her life and ours too," said he.

As he sipped his cup of tea and munched on ginger biscuits, Binodini realised that Shekhar was extremely garrulous and loved to talk...he spoke nonstop about his journey by ship...his stop at the various ports and of course cleansing of his sins in the holy Ganges.

"I am going to sue these donkey chaps in the Queen's court; he was as slow as a snail and god knows what he fed that animal it kept fouling up the air more than a factory chimney in Bristol."

Binodini could not help but giggle uncontrollably; she was soon joined by the Maharani and Beral Babu.

"Why don't us all take a break, the prince is seeing to all the arrangements for the pujo....I have not been to the Shiva mandir near the river for a very long time now," said the Maharani.

The idea was not bad at all; in fact, everyone agreed to it except for one.

Wiping bits of biscuit crumbs from his droopy moustache, Shekhar said, "It is an uphill task."

"Come, come brother do not be a spoilsport, you can always sit on Nestor."

Beral Babu's only pair of decent black pants was worse to wear even with the best darning and mending.....as if knowing about it, a selection of black and grey pants were laid out on the bed along with a few white shirts.

Binodini wore her long tweed skirt teemed with a heavy sweater, the Maharani was dressed similarly only her skirt had red checks, more concerned about the safety of the elder prince; the Maharaja stayed back and so did Khan.

Mishra was waiting with Gobordhan in the central courtyard, behind him stood Nestor all saddled up.

"Come sir, I will help you to mount," said Mishra.

Nestor seemed to be a horse with higher intelligence, each time Shekhar tried to mount him he would snort loudly and try to bite him....no amount of coaxing worked on the great beast....it seemed he could distinguish between riders according to their sizes. Maharani tried to help him by speaking sense into her horse but as Shekhar put one leg into the stirrup, he turned his great head and bit him in the posterior! Ouch! That must have hurt. Nestor was sent back to the stables but not before he got a stern warning from the Maharani.

That was it.... Shekhar could take no further such insults from such lowly beasts, he decided to walk. The day was cold yet with a bright sun and they had a pleasant walk till they reached the river after that they took a small meandering track that went uphill, though the slope was very gradual yet Shekhar came a huffing and a puffing....his groans and curses could be heard a mile away, Mishra being always the man of the moment devised a novel idea to deal with this problem two of the Maharani's guards tied a rope around his mid section and pulled him uphill.

The view from the top was breathtaking; after stretching out their legs for a short while they headed towards the mandir, the Maharani told them that it was almost five hundred years old and the Shivlinga lay deep inside the ground, on the top there was a large brass snake with shiny red eyes. Both she and Binodini performed pujo, offering raw milk and flowers.

By the time they returned back to the small square patch of grass on the hill side, the servants had set up mats to sit on and there was a large picnic basket waiting to be opened. People like Mishra look for people to scare and in Beral Babu, he had found an exemplary victim.

"Sir, you might be wandering why there is no pujari in this mandir....yes I am sure you do..." he said to Beral Babu who was munching a mouthful of cucumber sandwich. Hearing this, Beral Babu stopped munching.

"There is a large five-headed snake that roams these hills and guards the treasures of this temple....can swallow a man whole.... know what I mean," said Mishra with a wicked gleam in his eyes.

Beral Babu looked this way and that way as if expecting the snake to turn up from right behind the bushes. He somehow managed to gulp down the sandwich.

Shekhar who was sitting next to Beral Babu gaffed and laughed. "Next you will be telling us that the palace is haunted by a bunch of ghosts".

"Is it not?" said Mishra.

"Now that is enough Patta....no more of that," said the Maharani.

They returned to the palace happy and tired. There were no other mentionable incidents other than of course Shekhar's loud groans and curses while going downhill on his crow-like legs.

Before retiring to their beds that night, the Maharani took Binodini's hands in hers and said, "We have a busy day tomorrow sleep well. The protima of the Goddess Durga has arrived."

That night in bed, Beral Babu was reading an old leather bound book burrowed from the palace library.

"Have you found out about the Raibahadurs? Did you ask Mishra about his coming here?"

"I did they too are expecting him here for the pujo, but they do not know when he is going to come," he said a little thoughtfully.

"I hope Lady Sreelata is fine....we should go and look them up once we get back," she said with a bit of worry and concern in her voice.

"Yes we will, they both are such good and decent people and the amount of love and affection they have showered on us, I will always pray to god for their well-being."

"Do not worry so, let's sleep; I have been asked by the Maharaja to go with him to the treasury," said Beral Babu keeping his book down and pulling on the blue gold cord to turn off the lights of the chandelier.

The golden glow from the fire place made the room warm and cozy keeping out the cold evil fingers of the unknown that roamed the palace at night.

Two hooded figures stood before Bagha knowing the consequences of their failure.

"We did get past the guards but it is impossible to go anywhere near them they are never alone and with sacred fire burning in their room it is impossible."

Their blood curdling scream was heard by every passenger. Children sleeping in their mother's arms started crying, even the bravest of men were afraid to see outside their windows. The guards on the train were alert and started checking every boogey for the miscreant who had pulled the chain to stop it in the middle of nowhere, as they hurried towards the last of the coupes they heard a door open and bang shut but before they could react the train started moving.

One guard to another, "It has been almost a year now....every time the same thing."

"Who got down tonight....that too in the middle of nowhere? I suppose we never will know," said the second.

"The same thing happened about ten odd days back too," said a third.

"My grandfather was a station master during the Raj days; he spoke of riots and killings......the Maharaja and Maharani of this place died a gruesome death, the prince was hacked to pieces....very sad ending for the royal family," said the first guard pulling on his Indian leaf cigarette and blowing out thin spirals of smoke.

"Who killed them...British?"

"No not the British....in fact they were the apple of their eye....he is old; you know how old people are....talks about some Bandit king, crazy is it not?"

"You thing they are doing this," said a very young recruit shivering against the cold of the night.

"No mention of any of this to our sahib...I will kick your ass," said the first threateningly.

The guards moved on continuing their search, each knowing it was a futile exercise.

Mishra hurried to the Maharaja's presence; he looked angry and worried.

"Another attempt...."

"I am aware of it your Highness....stopped it just in time."

"Prince tells me you had to save Beral Babu's life in the forest....is he aware of the consequences?"

Mishra's silence was answer enough.

"Fate decides all...." said the Maharaja.

Mishra made his way through the winding passages of the palace, keeping a sharp eye. He was happy in his mind for making the right choices, he was glad that they had been able to rescue the elder prince....there was just one last task left....but there was an eternity for that....

14. A Royal from the Desert Kingdom

All were sitting outside in the lawn sipping coffee when the Maharani mentioned about the impending arrival of the Maharaja's sister.... Diya Devi, Rani of the Raja of Bhangarh. Both Mishra and Khan had gone to the station to receive her.

Shekhar who was sitting with his eyes closed on the armchair harrumphed out loudly and said, "Don't tell me so! By the kingdom of 'Thor' that parched stick is coming over....she is so dry that whatever rainfall that ever happens in that desert is all soaked up by her....they must have packed her off here to improve the biosphere....you know what I mean," winking wickedly at his sister.

His sister looked disapprovingly at her brother as she saw the Maharaja disliking the joke.

The Maharaja excused himself and asked Beral Babu to accompany him to the vault. After they finished their coffee, they all moved to a large hall near the mandir where the protima of the Goddess had been installed by the Raj Purohit. They all knelt on the floor and bowed down touching their forehead to the ground seeking her blessings.

Dressed in a red benarasi sari, the Goddess looked so beautiful and regal. Maids and other sahayaks of the palace were seen stringing flowers and mango leaves together.....the cooks of the palace had set up large chullahs in the courtyard and in huge kadais millk was being boiled to make various mishtis like rasmalai, jalebis, rasgullas, rabri, and the likes

The late morning sun saw the arrival of the Maharaja's sister. Mishra and Khan had gone to receive her from the station in the royal carriage.

Gobordhan was seen scurrying towards them, "Maharani Sahiba sahiba has arrived; carriage just reached the portico."

The Maharani on hearing that hurried towards the entrance of the palace followed by her handmaidens and Gobordhan…of course Binodini and Shekhar followed too.

Diya Devi was by no means any beauty, yet her tall and regal appearance made up for her lack of good looks, her hair cut fashionably into a bob and her light floral chiffon sari that floated around her stick thin figure, as one came into her presence one was overcome by very strong French perfume.

She gave a cursory peck on her sister in-laws cheek then turned her bead like eyes on Shekhar and said in a very strange thin voice "Oho! I see that Humpty Dumpty has already landed…don't crack your shell…..cannot be mended."

She spoke in crisp British English leaving Binodini a little nervous. Her luggage consisted of a large number of boxes and as Gobordhan and other servants started unloading, Shekhar started counting them loudly. "The desert people have at last realised their folly and packed you off…..now they can hope for some rain."

Beral Babu returned from the vault with a small wooden casket.

"The Maharaja asked me to give you this; it contains the jewellery for the goddess," said he to the Maharani.

"Come all of you help me out….we have the goddess to decorate," but just as she passed by Beral Babu, she came very close to him and spoke into his ears.

Beral Babu stood confused; for a minute he did not follow, remember what?….as it was the way had been long and difficult full of passages and doors, each step laid with caution because of the various bobby traps laid under the stones that could kill an unwary thief.

All waited for her in the saloon to freshen up and come downstairs, she came back after a short while in a billow of fragrance and chiffon, a servant followed her carrying a large suitcase.

Seated comfortably in a French love seat, she looked regal and stiff; Binodini was totally in awe of her, she opened her bag it contained presents for every one.....a gold jewellery box encrusted with pearls for the Maharani, a necklace for the prince, a toy box for the elder prince....he was the only person whose peck on her cheeks brought a faint smile to her thin lips. She carried a slimmer's guide for Shekhar.... he accepted his gift with a very comical bow and also thanked her for her thoughtfulness. Binodini was extremely surprised to receive a gift....it was a leather bound gold inlaid diary with a silver pen.

"Thank you so much, I am sure my husband will very much appreciate this gift of yours," said Binodini.

"What makes you think it is for him?" she asked raising her eyebrows an inch higher.

"....but I am not so very good at reading or writing," said Binodini very hesitatingly.

"It is never too late to start...is it not?" she said.

The pujo preparations were on under the strict supervision of the Raj Purohit, the dhakia played in the central courtyard. On the day of shoshthi pujo, everyone was up early in new clothes, the Maharani sat alongside with the Maharaja performing hom....offering dry fruits, incense and ghee into the sacred fire. Shekhar of course continued with his extreme polite comments and digs. Just as Diya Devi came up to put her offerings in the fire, he could not help himself at all and remarked. "Do not go too near the fire...dry things catch fire very quickly," with a wicked gleam in his eyes.

Food served kept to the lines of time bound traditions....there was sweet rice called Kanika, spicy tomato chutney with dates and Kismis, begunis which consisted of thin slices of brinjal dipped in gram flour paste and deep fried in mustard oil, and the traditional mixed vegetable curry cooked in mustard paste was mouth wateringly tasty. What Binodini liked the most was the sweet sour dal served piping hot.

The Maharani herself supervised the serving of the food to all the guests.....

Diya Devi displayed equal love for Shekhar, she was sitting next to him so she asked very politely, "Shall I serve you some dal...I am sure the well needs filling up."

Rising to the occasion gallantly, he said, "Please do not use a ladle to stir it; I would personally prefer a stick."

Watching their witty play of words, one would have thought of handing each of them a sword and they spar like professionals.

Day of Dashomi.....a frenzy of festivity was seen in the palace, food, sweets and more food....both Shekhar and Beral Babu freaked out, they had developed a common bond of friendship....both liked good food. Dhunuchi dance in front of the mother goddess was performed with great vigour....Beral Babu shed his inhibitions and joined the prince and Shekhar in the dance. Soft spirally clouds of incense sweetened the air with heavenly fragrance. Sindoor Khela.... the women folk of the palace all joined in, they applied red vermilion and haldi on each other...sign of goodness and purity of the soul.

That night as Binodini was packing in their room, Beral Babu who sat afar reading saw her looking extremely sad...he left the book and came close to her.

"Parting is a part of meeting, one cannot have one without the other, the wonderful experience that we have had...will always be treasured in our hearts.....love, respect, compassion and trust. Courage to tell the truth is what I have earned here, will last a lifetime."

Binodini hid her face in his chest and cried like never before.

"We celebrated pujo....just as the Raibahadur wished and I will let him know of that when we meet," said Beral Babu.

The next day, Maharani kept it very low key...Beral Babu went along with others for the emersion of the goddess.

A maid came running up to Binodini who was changing.

"Madam you are wanted in the mandir."

Binodini hurried downstairs...everyone was there. The Raj Purohit looked at the royal couple as if seeking their permission.

"We entrust this to you for safe keeping," he said.

"You are the guardian now," said the Maharaja

Binodini stood dumb founded, she looked at their faces….serious and sincere. Her hands were shaking. The saffron cloth wrap up lay heavy on her hands.

"Use it wisely when the time comes." Words kept ringing in her ears as she left the mandir.

It almost a quarter to nine the carriage was ready and waiting in the portico, Nestor was pawing the ground with his hooves ready to move, when….In the saloon, Binodini and Beral Babu took leave of everyone, touching the royal couple's feet seeking their blessings, the maharani blessed Binodini and taking off her string of black pearls she slipped it around her neck.

Shekhar hugging Beral Babu said, "We will meet again my friend… that I am sure off."

Diya Devi gave her customary stiff nod and said, "Do well."

It was a moonless night, the only light came from the lantern swinging from its post as Nestor put speed into his hooves. For a change Mishra was quiet…seeing Binodini tearful he did not relate any of his scary tales to Beral Babu.

Khan picked up their luggage and led the way.

The small station was dark and deserted no sign of the station master either. The whistle of the train could be heard at a distance.

The train engine let off great spirals of heat and smoke as it stopped with a great screech, Khan hurried inside with their luggage while Mishra helped Beral Babu and Binodini. Only a faint light of the lantern was seen as Binodini pressed her face against the glass of the window. The young strappy DCP of Kolkata Police, Avinash Bakshi, became alert the moment the train screeched to an unwarranted halt. He had cleverly placed constables in all the boogies….he was determined to catch the culprits who kept pulling the chain and stopping the train in the middle of nowhere…the sound of a door

opening was heard and a constable rushed to catch the culprit.....
when another constable past his prime hurried to inform his boss,
"Sir, we found Ramdin standing near the door....he is shivering like a
leaf and blabbering incomprehensively."

Another hurried in. "No sign of chain being pulled sir...."

The young DCP was agitated as his next promotion depended a
lot on solving this mystery and catching the miscreants, his boss won't
be pleased at all and how can the train be stopped without pulling the
chain?

"What about the driver?"

"Kept an eye on him sir....he also is bewildered."

The train had picked up speed, Binodini and Beral Babu settled
in for the night; a little while later, a young police officer came and
occupied the opposite bunk.

"Going to Kolkata?"

"So am I, nice to make your acquaintance Mr. Beral Chandra; by
the way, I am Avinash Bakshi, DCP, Kolkata police".

It was late, and soon, sleep overcame the weary travellers.

Binodini dreamt of a strange burnt figure......the face with cruel
red glowing eyes....hatred, vengeance.

Be warned someone spoke in her mind....she was again back in
the maze, the witches waiting for her return.

She has to protect her son....cannot let him come to harm.

She saw her husband wounded, his throat torn out by a pack of
wolves.....the prince holding the bowl to his lips....

She woke up frightened. She shook her husband who was sleeping
in the upper bunk. Seeing her so distraught he calmed her down.

"It is just a dream; it has no connection with reality, we have no
son remember?" he said gently.

For the rest of the night sleep was difficult to come, Binodini lay
awake thinking.

The water that she had drunk...had something to do with all this.

She so wanted to tell him.

She was too weak...how could she protect something so precious.

The two men hurried down the mountain side taking the meandering road. It was a bright sunny day. The tall iron gates lay wide open.

"I had locked these gates...I do not know who keeps opening them."

"You must have kept them open yourself you nit wit."

The main door of the palace too lay wide open...

"Vandals and drunks from the village, wait till I catch them."

The two men went inside. The air was cold, dank and musty. The great palace had fallen prey to neglect, cobwebs, and dust lay heavy everywhere.

"My grandfather used to speak of times when his grandfather was employed in the palace...these walls had paintings made in gold and decorated with diamonds, rubies, and emeralds."

As the two men moved about cautiously keeping a sharp lookout for animals both four- and two-legged ones, they came upon the staircase leading upstairs, years of neglect could be seen. "Do not step on the stairs....it will come down in a heap. Once there were crystal chandeliers here, now all that is left are bits and pieces of broken glass." The courtyard with red cobble stones had moss and grass growing in between.

"Look, there is murky green water in the fountain....but it has always been dry....it is indeed very strange."

The man stood wandering.....as to where all this water could have come from.

"Must have been the rain; what my sister saw in you I wander sometimes," said the other man shaking his head.

"Stop telling that...I feel very insulted."

"Really? you do have feelings?"

"Yes I do...I hate you speaking to me like that."

"Fine I will not in future....but I have a condition...if you drink this murky water, I will never tell you anything ever."

The two men stood glaring at each other. He would have done anything...to save himself from these daily insults. Cupping his palms he drank...surprisingly it tasted so good, he drank some more. The other man stood watching silently. He was now very sure that his sister had married a nutcase.

Cold vicious wind passed through the small dilapidated station, the train had stopped but the two had got away....

His men had become useless because of easy living...Bagha was furious. The whirl wind shook everything in its path as it passed. His time would come too........

15. Time after Time

It was a bright Sunday morning; Beral Babu was sitting at his writing desk, and he had kept his promise to the Maharaja…two letters a week. Binodini got him a cup of hot steaming coffee…black with cream. She stood next to him watching him write.

"There is never a reply," she said.

"There never was a promise of one," he said with a smile.

The doorbell rang. Binodini hurried away…her tuition teacher had come. She was studying for her intermediate exams, it had been quite a journey these past three years, and she had started her education from scratch.

Beral Babu called the servant and gave him the letter to post…

"Cannot go now babu; didimoni will be angry with me, she has asked me not leave the bedroom," said Gangaram.

"Do not worry so, I will sit here," said Beral Babu.

Making sure the mosquito net was secure, Beral Babu sat down with an English daily waiting for his wife to finish her studies. Looking at the bed he made a quiet mental journey, so much time had passed almost three years since Darimbari. A soft cry from the bed alerted him, drawing away the mosquito net he picked up his baby son all of two years of age, a bundle of joy in their lives.

That night during dinner, as Gangaram served them hot chapattis, Binodini asked her husband, "Any news about the Raibahadurs?"

"Not much…the servants do not know when they will get back…but yes I forgot to tell you I met their family doctor who had accompanied them to Germany. Lady Sreelata has recovered and doing well," said he in between mouthfuls.

Binodini listened to him fingering her string of pearls thoughtfully.

Sunanda, Tara and Suchitra came over the next day; the four friends chatted as usual over hot cups of steaming tea and pakoras served by Gangaram.

"I love the sari Binodini picked up yesterday from the sariwala… wish I had seen it earlier," said Tara.

"Even if you had seen it…none of us could have afforded it," said Sunanda.

"Yes you are so right…Beral Babu can afford it since he has become the manager of the bank," said Suchitra.

Beral Babu's day at the bank began early and he commanded respect among his men not only for his knowledge but also for his kind consideration for his juniors. Efficiency level at the bank increased due to Beral Babu taking personal interest and encouraging the race of Babu's to put in more effort and sincerity in their work. Devendra Ghosh of course learnt to spend more time on his own table completing his work. The man would often go around saying that he always knew that Beral Babu was meant for greater things….he would not stop at that….adding more flowery adjectives like Beral Babu's innate smartness, his slim appearance and of course his good taste in clothes.

Beral Babu did try to keep up his friendship with Badai da but the man simply avoided him and also changed his bus route.

Beral Babu travelled in the tram…he preferred the slow couch because by the time he reached home, he got enough time to read the English daily that he picked up at the stand and he was free to take his evening walk with Binodini by his side.

One evening, as they sat down to hot cups of black coffee with cream…Beral Babu handed a telegram to her. Rangamashi wanted to come over. Seeing her becoming a little quiet he smiled and continued, "I have written to her and informed that first I would ask you and let her know."

Binodini's exams were round the corner and she worked hard.

Rangamashi's visit would have to be postponed for the next year.

Life fell into a routine; Beral Babu was thinking along the lines of selling the house and moving into a better locality but Binodini, a creature of habits, did not wish to leave her safe haven where she had so many friends.

Selling off the scooter seemed very right, as it stood unused in one corner of the garden collecting rust and dust on its fenders. Samuel Culpeper, the previous manager was leaving India for good and his old Morris seemed a good affordable buy. Though Beral Babu still did suffer from road fear but with help of his old friend, the vet, he soon learnt to put the Morris into good use.

"Binodini has changed...I feel so," said Suchitra.

"She no longer falls much with our plans," said Tara.

Both friends sat quietly....each lost in their own thought.

One lazy Sunday morning, after a late breakfast, as Beral Babu was cleaning his car and Binodini was busy in the kitchen guiding Gangaram, the sound of horse hooves and the grinding crunch of iron wheels stopping in front the gate sounded so familiar...Binodini picked up her infant son and rushed outside.

Beral Babu was already speaking to the liveried messenger who handed him a small envelope and saluting smartly left.

It was an invitation to the Raibahadurs. "Get ready by four in the evening, hope I remember the way...I shall be driving with you as my co driver," said Beral Babu.

Beral Babu drove slowly yet steadily, the market place and shops gave away to broader roads that had wider pavements and were neatly lined with tall flowering trees, both were quiet lost in their own thoughts...it had been such a long time since they had met the Raibahadurs.

At last, they reached the tall majestic gates, the two large brass lions still at their posts. The little Morris reached the portico of the palace, liveried servants hurried down the steps and saluted smartly. They were led inside, the large elegantly decorated saloon was empty, the butler a short fellow clad in black pants and white shirt indicated to them to follow him further into the palace, the large saloon gave away to a smaller sitting room which had sofas and curtains in wine red…a small crystal chandelier added more white sparkle. The butler continued way past a small spiral staircase in brass and marble that led upstairs to a small balcony that housed rows of glass cabinets containing hard bound copies of many a precious first editions; he stopped in front of a large polished walnut wood door, gave a single knock and then turned the knob.

The room was small, yet, very tastefully placed. The heavy silk curtains in ocean blue complemented the gold white brocade of the period furniture, a large glass cabinet housed cut glasses and wine glasses on the topmost shelves while the wine bottles and other expensive liquor found a place on the slanting racks at the bottom, the fire place was unlit with a neat pile of logs, the walls were covered with white wall paper with tiny gold embossing of flowers; the walls were bare but for one single painting.

He was sitting near the fireplace with one foot raised on a foot stool…his feet was encased in a cast. The only other person in the room was the family doctor of the Raibahadurs. On seeing them, Raibahadur rose from the high-backed chair near the fireplace and hobbled on one foot; Beral Babu hurried to his side.

The two old friends hugged each other, then he turned towards Binodini who looked very elegant in a green silk sari that was complemented beautifully with a puffed sleeves blouse in similar colour. Her hair tied in a neat chignon and decorated with a small butterfly pin in silver.

"How are you madam? We are meeting after such a long time, it is such a pleasure," he said.

"The pleasure is all ours," replied Binodini.

Seeing her infant son in her arms…he was delighted taking the little boy in his arms; he excused himself and sat down.

"What name have you kept? He is such a handsome fellow…just like his father, who is so smart," said Raibahadur whose experienced eyes had not missed Beral Babu's transformation.

"We have named him 'Gajapati' after a very dear friend of ours," said Beral Babu.

"We returned just a few days back…and I was informed by the servants and my family doctor that you kept enquiring about us… that is very kind of you both," said the Raibahadur hugging the infant closer and playing with him.

"What happened to your foot?" Beral Babu enquired with concern in his voice.

"Just a small mishap on the horse; my good doctor here says it is just a hairline fracture."

Just then, the butler entered with a small tea trolley followed by Lady Sreelata. She still looked her amazing self but for a slight limp as she walked. She hugged Binodini and shook hands with Beral Babu, her delight and happiness new no bounds when she saw their infant son and taking him from Raibahadur's lap, she seated him on her own.

As they all sipped green tea, which had been brought all the way from China…they all appreciated the soft hint of mint in the tea. The doctor elaborated on the health benefits of drinking green tea every day.

After tea was over, the Raibahadur helped by the doctor hobbled over to a small writing desk in one corner of the room. Opening it he took out a large bundle of letters that was tied neatly into pile with a red ribbon.

Sitting down, the Raibahadur spoke with much thought behind what he had planned to say to his good friend. "Your letters got directed here to me….enjoyed reading them…each one of them but

at some point I realised that they were not meant for me...were they?"
He waited looking questioningly at Beral Babu.

Beral Babu shook his head, and with a little bewilderment said, "I wrote them to the Maharaja and Maharani who live in the palace."

The Raibahadur's bewilderment increased and he looked at the doctor in wonderment.

"There is no one living in the palace other than the caretaker," said the astonished doctor.

"Yes we met him...Patta Nath Mishra and of course Khan.... both trusted aides to the Maharaja and Maharani," said Beral Babu.

"Are you trying to tell me you both lived in the palace," asked the Raibahadur surprised with the very idea because he knew that the palace was not habitable at all.

"We celebrated pujo too....just as you wished," said Binodini happily, unaware of the effect her words would have on the others.

The Raibahadur, his wife and the doctor were left in bewilderment. Beral Babu too was at loss for words.

Binodini in her innocence kept speaking about the beautiful Maharani, Maharaja and the prince, the majestic beauty of the Hindol Kothi....how they had gone for picnics and the incident where the Maharani was bitten by a poisonous snake; she spoke about Nestor the majestic beast with three white hooves. The others, except for Beral Babu, were left dumbfounded and at loss for words that would spell sanity.

Lady Sreelata after some afterthought asked Binodini, "You are trying to tell us that you spent your holidays with all these people and you have really seen her?"

"I first saw her here at your home...she was standing at the head of the staircase," said Binodini excitedly as she kept fingering her string of black pearls drawing Lady Sreelata's attention to it.

"We have paintings of the horse you speak off....according to the paintings he has four white hooves," stated Lady Sreelata disbelievingly.

"What I saw I spoke off....I am not sure about your paintings," replied Binodini.

The Raibahadur did not know what to make of all this. The doctor, a man of science, too was confused because he knew that they both were not telling lies and the letters were a proof of that. But.... it did not fit into the rational pattern of thoughts that we humans have constructed for ourselves.

"I feel I must return these to you as they were not meant for me," said the Raibahadur, taking a deep breath.

They took leave off their hosts; the letters lay heavy on Beral Babu's hands as the doctor saw them off. The little Morris picked up steady speed as they left behind the palace grounds and entered the broad roads.

The doctor came back after seeing off the Raibahadur's guests, and saw the Raibahadur brooding over a glass of whisky.

"I do not know what to make of all this," said the Raibahadur.

"Even if they were lying....the letters written over a period of three years contradict that thought," said the doctor.

Just then, the butler came into the room. "Sir, the munshi seeks permission to meet you."

The munshi, groaning under the weight of a heavy file, waited for the Raibahadur in the study. How he wished he had left this job when he had, had the chance...now at this time of the evening he had been asked to come with all the old correspondences of the past three years.

Raibahadur went through the contents of the file with help of the munshi while the doctor kept him company. **At the end of the last pile, he came upon a telegram that contained only three words 'Guests No Come'.**

He showed it to the doctor....who drew deeply on his cigar as he read it.

That night after dinner, the Raibahadur's invited the doctor for a cup of coffee in the saloon. As Lady Sreelata made them cups of black coffee and added cream to it, she suddenly recollected something; keeping the pot of coffee down she got up in a hurry and went and stood near an old panting that hung in the saloon, her excitement knew no bounds.

"Come quickly both of you; see this."

The doctor helped the Raibahadur, and they both went and stood behind Lady Sreelata who was looking at an old painting of the erstwhile Maharani of Darimbari.

"Look here at this string of black pearls...I saw the same on Binodini," she said excitedly.

"I think you must be mistaken my dear," said the Raibahadur.

"I too agree with you on this, for there are only two such strings of pearls in existence...one that your ancestor wore but it was never found. The other lies in a vault in England in the possession of the Queen," said the doctor.

Lady Sreelata did not like being taken so lightly....

"What about the one I saw...it was...."

"A fake," said the Raibahadur trying to humour his wife.

The occupants of the small Morris were silent till they reached home.

Binodini hurried inside to feed her hungry infant, whereas Beral Babu parked the car, and while he was locking the doors, his eyes fell on the big bundle of letters lying on the back seat...picking them up he went inside.

During dinner that night, Binodini sadly said, "They think us to be liars...do they not?"

Beral Babu looked at his wife long and hard, and said, "Only God knows the truth."

The whole of next day, though Beral Babu did his best to concentrate on his work, he failed miserably; even Binodini had a tough time... the very thought of the Raibahadurs thinking of them as liars was hurting more than one could fathom. She busied herself cleaning the small aquarium in her sitting room, as she switched on the twin bulbs the rocks that her husband had got for her glowed and shown in the sand bed of the aquarium. Truth shows itself in many ways.

One evening, as both returned from their walk Gobordhan came hurrying up to the gate, and taking the baby's pram from Binodini's hands he informed them about their guest who had been waiting for them since the past hour and a half.

Wandering who it was, they walked in to find Binodini's distantly displaced cousin Shisir Biswas—a tall lanky young man, highly erudite but his displaced sense of great knowledge made others think of him as a little queer.

The pile of letters in Beral Babu's own hands lay open in front of him…he had utilised his hour of waiting well…one should say.

Beral Babu knew Shisir very, very well and his lack of common sense for respecting other people's privacy was indisputable. Beral Babu made an angry show of collecting the letters and putting them back in a neat pile.

"You should not read others letters, I think you are a little too big to be taught that," said Beral Babu in a huff.

Rebuff as these hardly affected the likes of Shisir and slid off like water from a drake's back.

"So many letters, whom have you been writing to? Absolutely amazing story you have here," said Shisir with total disregard to Beral Babu's anger.

"I have just started a printing business of my own…at the moment I am on the lookout for something worth printing…you have a landmine sitting here worth exploring," said he his eyes almost disappearing inside his eyebrows in excitement.

Shisir was as stubborn as a donkey and would not take no for an answer.

The first few copies had already hit the market….they sold off like hot cakes, the reviews and responses that the book received was just outstanding.

Life took a very dramatic turn for the Berals from this point on.

Almost every newspaper carried a review of his book and article on him.

A simple office babu who had worked his way up to the position of a manager of a bank had now acquired iconic status.....

He was a burning example for every common man who strived to dream big. The race of office Babus were made proud today....great deeds indeed.

16. Rise of a Phoenix

Badai da who was travelling by bus heard two men standing next to him discuss…

"You should read what he has written, simply fascinating, I could not keep it down till I had reached the last page and then I wanted to read some more," said the first.

"You are so right…hope he writes another book, he is a great writer," said the second.

A third man who heard the other two speak said, "My second cousin works in the same bank…I have a signed copy of his book."

Badai da could take it no more…he got off at the next stop. He so badly wanted to tell everyone he knew the great man more than anyone else but somehow such words got submerged in his heart when he recollected his nasty behaviour with Beral Babu.

Beral Babu had become a house hold name…his language and use of clever words were being compared by the entire literary world to likes of Dickens and Maugham.

With name and fame came unimaginable wealth and prestige. The top brass of the Swadhin Bank catapulted Beral Babu to the rank of a general manager since his mere association with bank had increased its importance and improved its image in the society by manyfolds.

Her husband's name and fame did not spare Binodini either; as the woman behind a successful man, she found her place rightly by his side. They attended book-reading sessions and travelled the length and breadth of the country giving lectures and attending conferences.

In the central headquarters of the Kolkata police a very important meeting was taking place, there had been too many disappearances of passengers and no bodies had been recovered so far.

"It is a matter of worry and concern sir…"

"It happens towards the middle half of the month…the train stops and the disappearances occur," said another senior officer.

"Chief, the officer you had sent for is here,"…said the orderly.

With a nod from the others who were at the meeting…he was shown into the room.

Avinash Bakshi was a smart young officer with a keen sense of 'Sherlock Holmes' like qualities and a daring attitude to explore the unknown.

"Let me introduce you all to my most able DCP, he is in charge of the case I was speaking to you all about," said the chief.

Pushing a hardbound book towards him across the table, the chief said, "Read this, it may help you in your investigations." Saluting smartly, Avinash Bakshi left the room.

"It has been a long investigation…we have not come up with much," said another senior officer.

"About three years back, we did come up with something but the incomprehensible blabber of a mentally disturbed constable cannot be taken seriously," said the chief.

Bakshi left the police headquarters with mixed feelings…it had been three long years and yet the mystery deepens more. Bakshi a man of fixed habits…four in the evening one would find him in the riding club playing a rough game of polo for at least an hour but on that day he did even come for his appointed game with his other police cronies instead he sat reading the book till about four in the morning.

Writers are but spinners of magical webs to enthrall their readers…on cannot make such imaginations the basis of any police investigation….though he did agree that the book was indeed good.

One evening as Binodini was reading an article in the English daily and Beral Babu was playing with his son…Gangaram brought in a sleek looking white envelope and handed it over to Binodini.

As Beral Babu gave her a questioning look, she read out from the card inside. Dolly D. Banerjee, a reporter with the Revolving Daily

Times, wanted to interview them both and was seeking an audience.

"No matter how many interviews you give they still want more," said Binodini with a satisfied smile.

Dolly D. all of thirty years of age belonged to one of the old well-known families of Kolkata, studied abroad most of her life, spoke fluent British English and a smatter of accented Bangla. Adventurous by nature she had, had share of adventures with the opposite sex but sometimes such adventures do backfire. Nursing a broken affair she had landed back home and had been working as a journalist of some sorts.

Her boss, a balding homely man, wanted an exclusive scoop for his paper…who better than Dolly…. of course.

Saturday was just round the corner and Dolly spent long hours in her office doing a thorough background work on the writer and his wife. Mr. Beral Chandra was not only very knowledgeable but extremely sharp in his dealings; hence, one needed to be extra careful, whereas his wife, though reputed to be a sweet and polite person, was also extremely well read….she too had written a book of short stories for children which had been very well received by her young audience. Running her long red-tipped fingers through her short curly hair, she started to think on what she would ask in her interview the next day.

Well prepared she drove down to the writers well-appointed Bungalow in one of the most exclusive areas of Kolkata. No photo could do justice to such a beautiful house; it was more like a small chateau than a bungalow, the liveried guards at the gate after verifying her identity let her in. Large green lawns framed by a riot of flowering plants, a small fountain with a cupid at its centre and flocks of fan tailed doves that flew in a small cloud as she drove past. The house was old and built out of grey stone, creepers and vines with tiny orange red flowers lent colour to the otherwise dull grey walls.

The house did not have a portico but it had a large fort-like entrance, and once Dolly got out of her car, she had to climb up the red sandstone stairs to reach the main door that was massive with a large bell-like knocker.

A well dressed servant in crisp dhuti and punjabi guided her in. The house had a rustic charm…during her visit abroad she once had the chance to visit a duke's castle…its rough rock hewn walls and fireplaces had really captured her liking. The floors were also in grey matching the outer walls but expensive Turkish rugs and Kashmiri carpets lend a riot of colours. The furniture was in heavy polished walnut with silk cushions of different colours, beautiful and rare paintings adorned the walls, the windows had been kept open to let in the sweetened air from the garden.

Once seated she clicked a few photos…the waiting was short. The writer was a tall and slim gentleman looking extremely at home in his hand stitched black cords and white shirt, his wife was so elegant…her long hair in a loose braid, wearing a crisp ocean blue colour cotton sari with a French lace blouse—she looked extremely alluring.

Between cups of tea, she interviewed the couple. Then she requested for a few photographs in the garden, and between photographs, she kept on her barrage of intelligent questions.

"Your story…is it all imagination?"

"What do you think as a reader?" said Beral Babu.

"What about the cave? Does it really exist?"

"Of course it does…an average small mountain will have dozens of such caves," he said.

"Can I see the stones you got for her?" Dolly asked trying not to look too eager.

"You mean the gems…of that size won't I be foolish to keep them in my aquarium…in case I did possess such gems wouldn't I keep them safely in a vault?" said Binodini with a mischievous smile.

"What about the magic bowl?" asked Dolly praying hard in her mind that the writer would slip out some clue and she would get her scoop.

"Do you sincerely think that such a bowl exists?" Binodini shook her head smiling. "Our readers love to believe everything they read; the other day I was at a party and someone asked me about my string of black pearls."

Both of them laughed aloud and Dolly D. also joined in but she was a determined young woman not to give up easily.

The palace and the small little station that you have written about, are they real....I mean do they exist?" she continued.

Beral Babu cast a knowing look at Binodini.

"As real as you and me," said Beral Babu.

The next day, an extensive interview appeared in the Revolving Daily Times.

"Look our Binodini's photo...she looks so amazing," said Tara who had come over to Sunanda's house for tea.

"Seen her house...they brought this house from the royal family of Jessore," said Suchitra.

"Say we all go and meet her...but one is hesitant you know," said Tara.

Sunanda who had been sitting all this while quietly listening to everyone said, "As far as I know our friend...she may change outwardly but inside she is still the same person.... of that I am very sure."

Dolly D. was very satisfied with her work but her very homely balding boss was not so easily satisfied.

In a very nasty loud tone he said, "Is this the scoop I had sent you for? This is stale news; wake up Miss D. I want an exclusive, know what I mean.?"

Dolly drove back home with a heavy hand, not very happy with the present state of things in her life. Dinner was a lonely affair...her sisters-in-law busy with their own lives.

The old deaf maid in her house was the only one around to serve her dinner.

She re-read the morning paper and tried to read between the lines;

suddenly a mad idea hit her...leaving her dinner, she ran to book a call.

Gangaram answered the phone; poor fellow stood no chance against the persuasive female voice at the other end.

"Why has she called up, at this hour?" Binodini did not sound very pleased.

Beral Babu took the call in his study.

"You have called me up at this hour, is it something urgent?" he sounded stern.

"Please...I am sorry but my life depends on your answer," said Dolly D. trying to sound soulful in order to get her way with the eminent writer and it did work.

"Did you ever go back there? I mean...."

"No...."

Then there was silence at the other end and the writer hung up.

It was just about closing on upon nine...if she would hurry, she could still board the train. Stuffing a few necessary items into a small duffle bag and picking up her camera, she ran out and hailed a taxi.

The old deaf maid not knowing why the young unmarried girl of the house was leaving at this indecent hour, ran upstairs to wake up the master of the house.

She just about managed to reach the station in time to see the train chugging in. The first class coupe that she was travelling in was vacant. A little while later, a very smart police officer came and sat down in the opposite bunk.

Dolly, very smart in the ways of men, was soon opening a conversation, which was to her benefit of course.

Smiling at him in a slightly friendly way, she soon drew his attention. Though the officer was very much a married man with two kids, men are but men; they slip and fall as they go.

"I think I have seen you somewhere?" he said.

"Yes you must have, I am the same reporter from the Revolving Daily Times and I had come to the police headquarters the other day…I am Dolly D. with a dot and here is my card."

Taking the card from her hand and without even glancing at it, he said, "Yes of course, I do recollect, now that you have mentioned it and ah! yes, where are my manners, I am Avinash Bakshi, DCP, Kolkata Police."

The journey had become quiet enjoyable for the young officer and Dolly; a sharp and extremely manipulative woman that she was, she knew she could get something out of the officer.

The next day after evening hours, Dolly noticed that quite a number of sharp-eyed constables had been placed at various exits on the train. Her sharp senses alerted, she kept an eye on the on goings. The DCP too was no longer to be seen….she waited with baited breath and prayed for something to happen.

It was a little before midnight when suddenly the train which was travelling at full speed came to a screeching halt. She heard heavy booted footsteps and alert commands; just then she heard a door open and close with a loud bang…throwing caution to the winds, she followed.

The train moved within a few seconds of stopping. A posted constable had seen her getting down and immediately ran to his superior to report.

Immediately the chain was pulled and the train was stopped. The DCP and his constables, well-armed and with powerful search lights, got off the train.

"At this time of the year one does not expect such thick fog," said the DCP to the sub inspector who was following at his heels.

The fog moved about in swirls engulfing the men in uniform; visibility was poor just a few feet even with such powerful search lights. Thorny bushes, potholes and sharp rocks made the going difficult. The men searched for the missing reporter for over an hour, a constable stumbled and fell down into a large ditch as he was scrambling out he found something…immediately he informed his superior and handed over his find.

The passengers had been alerted to the danger and had been asked to stay in groups and under no circumstances to get off the train. Some who were a little more courageous than the others did try to see what was happening by pressing their faces against the windows but the thick fog made visibility almost next to nil.

Finding nothing, the DCP returned to the train with half of his men. Planning to come back with reinforcements, he stationed the other half there so that in case of requirement the men could be easily mobilised.

As the train chugged away, a world of solitary silence descended upon the men. Though winter was still a little further away, yet, the men felt the cold and clammy hands of the fog engulfing them in its chocking embrace.

The sub inspector, an experienced man in his field, realised here on this night that he was dealing with something that was beyond his field of vision, keeping his men together for safety.

The cold had become oppressing and almost unbearable one could see the men breathing out funnels of vapour.

They all sat close together in the small shed…alert with weapons cocked. The sub inspector kept talking to his men boosting their morale and he kept a fire going throughout the night.

The fog kept a thick cover of blanket upon them like a relentless sentinel covering the heinous crime committed.

Before the early morning sun could rise the DCP returned with reinforcements and sniffer dogs.

Alas! But even after four hours of search there was no sign of any body or otherwise….

It seemed as if the reporter had disappeared into thin air.

The dogs too behaved extremely strange, after a particular point they would just go round in circles and again come back to the same point from where they had started.

Collecting whatever little evidence that he could find, the DCP decided to give up the search....

17. An Unsolved Mystery

The chief was extremely unhappy with the way the whole affair had turned out to be, especially a disappearing reporter that to from a well-known family of Kolkata who had connections in the political circles...the press was after their blood. Police incompetence and careless attitude were the headlines of the paper.

Bakshi with a sense of sniffing out the truth was not to be taken lightly...he paid a visit to the reporter's work place and came to know about her keen interest in the eminent writer's work and also came to know about her recent write up in the paper.

At her home, the situation presented was totally different, while her sisters-in-law painted her as a very colourful personality and seemed happy that she had disappeared, her brothers maintained stoic silence. The deaf maid was of great help for she kept picking up the phone and speaking into it...this made him pay a visit to the telephone exchange.

Avinash Bakshi hurried to the police headquarters...he had a small package in his hand. The chief seemed unhappy with him but once he saw this.... he would have to change his mind.

"Avinash, you are one of my best but I also have superiors to answer to..." started the chief.

"Sir, I wish I could change what has happened but I have a hunch she had planned it all along to go down there...we found her camera... she had used up most of the reel."

"In our line of work we do not go by hunches...I must tell you that, you have to do better than that," said the chief.

"I am well aware sir, that is why I have got a copy of the phone records on the night she left her home...her last call was to the residence of the eminent author," said the DCP.

"I see…these writers spin a web of fantasy and people are so taken in by it all," said chief looking at the sheets of typed paper.

"I feel sir she was investigating the disappearances and also connecting it to the book," said the DCP.

"I am getting your point now…anything else?" the chief asked seeing the package in his hand.

"These are the developed photos…I could not make any sense, might be the fog or the night shadows…I am not sure sir," said the DCP passing the developed prints into the other's hand.

The chief went through them not once but twice, shaking his head in disbelief.…those photos contradicted the rational belief of man.

"These should not fall into the wrong hands…let the CBI decide future course of action, it is beyond us now.…" said the chief looking extremely thoughtful.

As the young DCP saluted smartly and turned to leave the chief called him and said, "Great job, keep it up."

Binodini read the news about the missing reporter…she remembered her coming over to take their interview.

Beral Babu returned home after a few days…

"She asked me a very strange question on that night when she had called me up," said Beral Babu a little thoughtfully.

"You should have warned her…" said Binodini.

"We have a promise to keep…no matter what the cost," he said.

The case was passed over to the CBI.

Nothing much is known about it…the evidences were presented before the governor.

After a closed door meeting of the high ups, the case was closed in order to prevent unnecessary panic among the citizens.

Almost forty odd years have passed.…

Two men hurried down the small meandering track on the hillside—one young and handsome, the other old and withered with age.

"Hurry up you old fool; I do not have the whole day....god knows why I still put up with you," said the younger man.

Grinding his teeth angrily the old man tried to increase his pace... God knows what his sister had seen in this devil's son of a man.

"What has happened? Cat got your tongue? Are you not going to say I will ring your scrawny neck?" said the younger man and laughed aloud.

On reaching the palace grounds, they made their way in....

The two men sat outside in a small clearing in front of the small house of the munshi of Hindol Kothi...smoking on a common Hookah. The wife of one comes out with a plate of savoury for her brother who was visiting them after a very long time. Giving him a smile she pointed out to her grandchildren playing in the palace grounds. Her back now bent with age, her hair a dirty white, she was but just a shadow of the beautiful woman that she once was.

She looked at her brother who had also withered with age and then at her husband, who stood up suddenly to shout at his grandchildren who were throwing stones at the family pet...a small white cow. The other two looked at him in wonderment.

He still looked like what he did forty odd years back; the vagaries of nature had missed him altogether.

On such dark nights when the fog settles thick on the ground... the train still stops with a grinding crunch...heavy booted footsteps are still heard... looking and searching...be warned not to get tempted to step out for.....

THE END

www.ingramcontent.com/pod-product-compliance
Lightning Source LLC
Chambersburg PA
CBHW050144110726
47898CB00008B/2657